About the Author

The author describes her idea of a perfect way to unwind is to curl up under a blanket in front of the fire and get completely lost in a novel. She loves to journey into other cultures through travelling the globe and especially exploring unique cuisines – taking home what she has learnt and demonstrating this in her own cooking.

In her day to day life, she has achieved two master degrees and works in international education. This allows her to pursue another passion of hers which is supporting international students globally to achieve their very best, strongly believing – these students are the next generation to shape our world for a better future.

Maverick

Aurora Stone

Maverick

Olympia Publishers
London

www.olympiapublishers.com
OLYMPIA PAPERBACK EDITION

Copyright © Aurora Stone 2023

The right of Aurora Stone to be identified as author of
this work has been asserted in accordance with sections 77 and 78 of
the Copyright, Designs and Patents Act 1988.

All Rights Reserved

No reproduction, copy or transmission of this publication
may be made without written permission.
No paragraph of this publication may be reproduced,
copied or transmitted save with the written permission of the publisher,
or in accordance with the provisions
of the Copyright Act 1956 (as amended).

Any person who commits any unauthorised act in relation to
this publication may be liable to criminal
prosecution and civil claims for damage.

A CIP catalogue record for this title is
available from the British Library.

ISBN: 978-1-80439-287-4

This is a work of fiction.
Names, characters, places and incidents originate from the writer's
imagination. Any resemblance to actual persons, living or dead, is
purely coincidental.

First Published in 2023

Olympia Publishers
Tallis House
2 Tallis Street
London
EC4Y 0AB

Printed in Great Britain

Dedication

For all those who fight for forever love in the same way – with wildfire in our hearts

Acknowledgements

Thank you to each and every person who guided, encouraged and supported me to become the person I am today. You walk alongside me on my journey and inspire me each and every day. You know who you are and I am eternally grateful x.

Maverick

I silently seethe as I wake to the sound of Matt Corby 'Brother' blaring through the speakers less than two meters from my head.

I'm dazed and blurry, a familiar and yet entirely unwelcome feeling.

My head is heavy, and my eyes feel like they have been sand blasted after a dramatic walk through the sirocco winds, as they wildly cross through the vast plains of the Sahara. Now that would actually be like a walk through a well-manicured, picturesque type 'Pleasantville' in comparison to the chaos that is me.

I am coherent enough to realise the concurrence behind the song I've just woken to and my miserable state of existence. I shift slightly; I'm lying somewhere extremely uncomfortable.

A bitter coldness sweeps over me, it is as if I spent the night camping in a tent where an uninvited frost has silently seeped inside the tent and settled into my bones overnight. What started out as an exciting adventure is now an experience I would rather politely pass on next time. The difference is – I am not camping, my arm is completely numb, and I am desperately cold, not from a normal nature experience but rather my drug induced sleep on the floor.

Unfortunately for me there is no polite pass on this adventure, this is my life.

My arm is entirely senseless from the angle I've been sleeping and I'm angry I even woke up as I close my irritated eyes and wonder why even the music hates me today. The melody reaching my ears is a musical reminder of all the dreadful, fucked up things I've done.

My brain stirs and questions start to formulate as to my most recent location and the events leading to this painful pounding in my head. I strain to slowly roll over with my eyes squinting at the low wooden table in front of me, it's glazed with drug paraphernalia, tobacco spread between the discarded cans, stale chips crushed into the surface and smears of something entirely unworthy of my attention any longer.

My back presses against something solid and unmoving, an object that groans a long awful sound and I silently curse. A hand reaches between my shoulder blades cementing the knowledge that there is a body behind me. I have no intention of finding out the owner of the body, yet I'm determined to move from this position to restore some sort of feeling back into my limbs and take stock of the situation.

I roll over, slowly capturing an image of the owner of these sounds. She has dark long, wavy hair, it is messy and sprayed out behind her. Matching her dark sunken eyes, black mascara streams down her face as she slowly opens her eyes and stares directly at me. Her glassy eyes bore straight through me as she stares with an uninhabited and vacant look. "Her eyes remind me of a dark and hollow place, perhaps showing me my own reflection." I consider silently.

She closes her eyes as I continue to inspect her. Her cheeks are gaunt and pale with perfectly shaped lips albeit the pinkish smears of lip stick, left behind from a night of mayhem.

I attempt to focus harder and push the fog from my scrambled brain as I concentrate on the lifeless form beside me.

"She could be beautiful," I think to myself, frowning at the thought of her stupidity waking up next to me. "I am an asshole," I think to myself.

The nights events skim my mind; a bombardment of faceless people race through my head, drugs rampant in the occupants creating a boundless amount of regret as I'm flooded with memories, alcohol consumed freely as laughter and 'deep' conversations that have little to no value in everyday life reach their peak, and finally my constant need to forget, the feeling of pain and emptiness swallowing me like a cavernous black hole until finally nothing, an endless nothing.

I close my eyes as a voice shouts above the music; the sounds pierce the air, jolting me with a sharpness that adds to the relentless pounding in my brain.

"Maverick, Mav!" they are screaming my name.

"Mav, can you hear me? Maverick man, you need to run now!" the panicked voice screams at my lifeless body on the floor, shaking me, urging me to do something I don't think I'm entirely capable of in that moment.

I sense a scuffle and feel the full force of a blow to my head and back before I can even turn to see the imminent threat, one that was apparently approaching rapidly. Based on the urgent screaming for me to run seconds ago, I assume that threat is entirely too close as a body shoves me down sharply into the floor face down, knees digging into my spine whilst my hands are pulled at an awkward, yet again all too familiar angle, as they are cuffed roughly behind my back.

I am rendered immobile. A heavy weight remains on my back with the force taking my breath away as I am subdued. "Fuck," I bite out as I struggle with the notion that I do not want to be trapped and I most certainly do not want to be in this position at this moment.

My body fails to put up any kind of resistance apart from a brief shuffle of my arms. I am strong, but the effects of months of drug and alcohol abuse renders me powerless against the force arresting my body. It could have been a twelve year-old arresting me right now and the outcome would likely be the same, no need for the forces finest to arrest me. "Let's send our weakest link to collect Maverick." I laugh internally and this brings a smile to my face as I conjure the images in my head.

My senses jolt back to life as I tune back into the mayhem that surrounds me. It feels like rotating the old radio dial to find the station that you want. As you slowly turn the knob, the static and crackling dissipates and the sound becomes clearer and clearer until you are satisfied the quality is perfect and the dial can now rest in that position, its job is done.

The sounds in the room assault me; people are screaming. I hear the shuffling of shoes across the old rickety timber floor, the stomping on the rubbish left over from the long nights and the verbal threats being slung in all directions.

I suck in a deep breath and stop struggling as I hear those painful words resonate deeply again. "Maverick Black, you are under arrest, anything you say can and will be used." I shut it out. I switch off and in that moment the fight drains out of me like an inky blackness seeping out my body, deciding I'm no longer worthy of the evil fight we wage together each night.

My life is slowing ebbing away from me and I feel myself slipping further off the broken ledge I've placed myself on. I am ashamed, I am angry and worst of all I am broken. Fog and hate consume my brain as I am pushed to my feet and waded through a swarm of people.

My brain is moving so fast but I can't quite catch anything. It is similar to orienteering, although I can see the brightly coloured flags, they continue to slip through my grasp each time I get close enough to feel the fabric slide into my hands.

I feel myself being roughly shoved into the car, hands pushing my head under the door and into the seat, slamming me back to the present and fuelling my anger even further.

I pass the drive in a furious silence, deciding not to even ask my alleged crimes this time. "What the fuck does it matter anymore?" I inwardly sigh, "I just want to be alone. Why won't the world let me go?"

Maverick

"Mr Black, can you hear me? It's Detective Ryland. I need to ask you a few questions?"

"Fuck off," I reply. I'm furious now that I've been woken again, this time handcuffed in an interrogation room of the local police department.

I'm bleary and uncomfortable, oddly though I managed to drift off to sleep with my head bowed into my arms and my body slumped over the table. "Sleep is what I need," I think to myself, days of endless sleep. The kind of sleep where there is nothing, just darkness and the opportunity to be completely alone, be at peace and importantly, unaware of the world passing by.

"Very well," replies Detective Ryland, interrupting my dreams of future sleep in which I imagine is beckoning me with a frail hand. Over and over the hand motions, calling me to join them like a siren call, one I cannot ignore and one that is so welcoming it entirely takes over my brain as the only direction I need to go.

"Would you like me to call someone for you?" His voice interrupts my internal ramblings, filled with genuine concern for my wellbeing. "Interesting," I think. It is his job to play the hard line with the suspects, make the difficult decisions and ultimately has the power to change the course of someone's life. In this scenario I ponder whether he is playing a very good game of good cop or he has someone is his life like me, someone he cares for deeply and hence empathy cannot escape him in here with me.

Minutes pass in silence.

Detective Ryland sighs. "Look Maverick, I have seen you in here too many times to count, I want to help you. You just need to let me," he pleads.

"No," I reply flatly as I stand and in the same breath push the table forcibly away from me, an act of defiance once again.

I don't know why I did it, it is not like I can magically leave this room. I am handcuffed and trapped here and he is messing with my fragile mind as I replay the words he just spoke in my head over and over.

"You can't help me. No. One. Can," I emphasise. My voice strong and steady now as I release that statement. I push everything; every emotion, thought and feeling away from me in that moment and store them in a dark catacomb, never to be unearthed and stare back at him.

Normal people would want to observe their surroundings, 'What is the room like? How big is the room? Where are the exits? What colour are the walls?' anything to give themselves purpose in that moment. I on the other hand – have no purpose and therefore everything in the room, including Detective Ryland, is irrelevant.

Hands push me gently back into my seat as I continue to stare defiantly at Detective Ryland, his eyes downcast in that moment and I consider the fact that without a doubt – this is one battle he will not win.

He appears a strong man with a solid, toned build and sharp features exposing small scars that litter his hairline like a branding. His age lines are only slightly apparent, you need to look closely to observe them but they are there. Worn by someone who has more than likely seen a myriad of sinister acts in his journey and if I was not mistaken, even participated in those in his youth with his biker gang vibe radiating from him.

I would have assumed he was part of a biker gang were it not for the official badge hanging round his neck; declaring him an upstanding member of the community – to protect and serve. "He could easily pass for the president of such club," I consider as I inspect the tattoos artfully etched into his arms.

Black sharp angry lines snake up his arms and under his sleeves which are effortlessly rolled up at his elbows, his hair is light and closely shaved on one side with sharp wild blonde cuts left untamed on the other. His eyebrow ring gives him an air of mischief and defiance about him and I'm left wondering if that is a hazard in his line of work. I am confident though, no matter how concerned this detective appears to be, he could put me down instantly without hesitation – "a man highly trained in areas they dare not teach at the police academy." I assess silently.

I concede defeat and slowly slink back into my chair as the detective slides the paper across the old worn, musty blue table directly in front of me. "Okay, here's your court summons Maverick. Your due in court on the 25th September at ten a.m. on charges of theft and aggravated assault." He pauses and raises an eyebrow in my direction.

He is searching for any kind of response, a reaction that would demonstrate I am not impenetrable, illicit a response that I care about my future and I will take the olive branch he is giving me. Instead, I remain unmoving, unaffected by his words and sit perfectly still and in silence as he continues. "You will be released from our custody in twelve hours unless someone posts bail for you, whichever comes first."

I look up at Detective Ryland leaning over the table and my hard stare turns to a smirk, the edge of my mouth moves slowly upwards and my dark eyes focus as I speak directly to him.

"Well, I guess we're having Sunday date night together then as No. One. Is. Coming. For. Me. Ever," I reply slowly.

"Sunday?" replies Detective Ryland as he shakes his head in defeat. "Mav, it is Thursday." He stands and leaves the room as I am left to deal with the mental blow he just unwittingly and cruelly dealt me.

It is entirely too much to process for my fucked up fragile mind. "How could I lose four days? Where have I been?" I ask myself quietly as I slowly and reluctantly absorb the sadness that engulfs me.

I stand in the tiny cell and observe myself in the small mirror fixed to the wall. Grime covers the outside of the mirror, it is blatantly obvious dirty hands have moved countless times across the mirror surface in attempts to sharpen the image of the reflection.

I attempt to peer through the grime as there is not a chance in hell I am touching that mirror. There must be some form of self-preservation left in me I wonder with that thought. "I wake up frequently in unknown places, dirty infested hell holes with the lowest of society and yet I refuse to touch a dirty mirror?" A hilarious thought in my fucked-up brain as my dark, jet-black hair sweeps in front of my face.

I scruff the back of my neck and run my hands through my hair hoping to feel a little more alive. I tousle the short messy strands at the back of my head and smooth the front over the left side of my face. I move closer to the mirror and roll my eyebrow ring around slowly back into place, attempting to chip off the dried blood encased around the ring.

"From what part of my adventures caused this latest cut near my eye? Was it today? Last week?" I sigh to myself as I struggle to re-call what event lead to this destruction. I have zero memory of the incident so my useless attempts to restart my tired brain are a wasted energy. "It doesn't matter. What's done is done. What will be. Will be," I reflect silently to myself as I splash cold water over my face and attempt to focus on my image again.

My eyes appear in the reflection, large and dark yet so empty, like a hollow abyss staring back at me. My face reflects, chiselled and strong as I observe myself through the smudges in silence. Pierced through my lip is a small silver ring which curves perfectly around my lip, encouraging a smirk at the memory. It was more of a novelty toy than a fashion statement as I remember my mother's face when I returned home with it at seventeen years old, brandishing my new asset. Mum paled, bringing her hands to her face and said, "Ohh my beautiful boy, why have you mangled your face? You are already beautiful to me." I laugh out loud, smiling at the fact she thought I was trying to beautify myself.

My smirk fades away and pain invades me as I try to remember how long it has been since I've seen her. Deep inside I feel my whole body convulse with a crushing feeling. It's hard to breathe. I miss her with my entire being, although the pain of returning home is too much. "What have I done?" I curse myself as I lay down and curl myself into a ball on the cold hard bed, clasping myself for warmth.

I fall asleep in the tiny cell as a silent tear falls down my face.

Isabelle

The sun beams brightly though my window as I shift uncomfortably in my single bed.

I sit upright and look out the window through my faded makeshift curtains. They don't block out the morning light as you would expect curtains to do, but it was the best I could do with the minimal resources I had.

I tirelessly made them myself from the thin blue cotton sheets I found, stuffed into one of the drawers in the hut when I arrived on the island.

"It is going to be another scorcher today," I think to myself. "I need to get up, the sand is stinging my legs and I'm sweating uncontrollably and it is only seven a.m. Thirty days since I've tortured myself in this beautiful hell hole and one hundred and fifty two days since my life was ruined." I sigh.

I get up out of bed and wander slowly out to the front porch in my thin cotton shorts and singlet. "This place is only temporary, a brief stop." I remind myself as I shuffle outside, past the empty cans and bottles strewn lazily across the worn plastic table and faded timber decking. I grab a water from the mini fridge sitting on the front porch to quench my thirst and head back inside my tiny hut to prepare for another day in hell.

I change my sheets in silence, the sand fills my bed every night regardless of whether I've been to the beach or not. I'm living on a secluded island off the coast of the mainland; no phone, no television, no luxuries, and no unwelcome stares or whispers as I walk around the university campus, so this hell is home for now but it seemed to tick all the right boxes when running away.

"Hell is much better than life at home with my past haunting me relentlessly." I cringe internally as a bombardment of painful memories flood back to me in this moment. I shake them off, firmly jamming them back away in a tiny locked box inside my brain and give myself a pep talk. It is certainly not as peppy as a cheerleader would approve of, but I am trying as I mentally file through the next steps of the 'Isabelle Mission', as I like to refer to it. "Harden up (not on track), afford the journey home (in progress), decide your next steps (not on track)." I consider these steps to myself, a little more deflated after realising the mission still only has three very basic items, and only one of them is currently barely achievable in my fragile mind.

The past thirty days on the island 'hell' as I more affectionately refer to it, has actually been a positive step for me. Each day I am starting to think a little more clearly as I feel the haze slowly start to fade away that has blanketed my brain for so long. This may be my survival instincts kicking in while I'm here, but I have this overwhelming and persistent urge telling me I need to try. Try harder to; pick myself up, wear my scars like a badge of honour, straighten my invisible crown and be stronger.

It is although the island has given me a new chance. A new opportunity, slowly clearing the fog in my jumbled brain, and forcing a stop to the blurry memories I was unwillingly creating – each minute, each hour, of each day.

My memories are hazy, like a dark nimbus cloud that blocks everything out and leaves my thoughts stuck in an endless void, making it incredibly difficult to retrieve even one. It is too painful to try and believe me, I have tried. I'm sure a qualified professional would have a proper term or explanation for this, but I will never know. I will never tell another soul these feelings, nor the feelings I had before the dense fog lifted, for which I hide the permanent scars each day very carefully.

I dress in my brown hessian shorts paired with my blue and yellow beach theme tank top, the staff all wear the same theme regardless of department, but I've never understood the itchy hessian shorts in the sweltering weather. "Perhaps it's meant to add to the beachy theme on the island by resembling coarse sand," I think as I struggle to manage my wild shaggy hair.

My hair is blonde and long, but with a lack of hair care and no hair straighteners here on the island, it seems to have taken on a wild life of its own. I smile though as I tie it up, it feels like it's a new part of me – wavy beach free hair to represent the new carefree spirit I'm pretending to exhibit to my new colleagues and hut neighbours on the island.

The island holds around two hundred and fifty staff at a time. All staff are housed on the island and discreetly hidden away from the elite and privileged guests who frequent here all year round, paying thousands of dollars for peace, tranquillity and relaxation.

The staff on the island are a diverse group of people, but ultimately all here for the same reason – everyone is running from something. Career progression and life experience as a reason for moving here could be considered a lie, far from the truth of why we are all actually here. I fell in the latter group as soon as I arrived; all smiles and ready for my 'life experience'.

I had just celebrated my twenty-first birthday. I was halfway through my third year of university and life was supposed to be a well-planned, well executed future model. It all fell apart, and I fell apart – in the most grand, dramatic spectacular way that would put even the most absurd burlesque performance to shame. "So here I am, gaining some 'life experience'," I laugh to myself, knowing there are others who have arrived here with the same adventurous motto. Yet I see them, and I see straight through their transparent facades, as sadly – we all alike.

Everyone is running.

Arriving on the island you are scrutinised by the staff; inspected, prodded, questioned and eventually released to choose your own path if you make it that far. The staff turnover here is three hundred and sixty five staff members per year – one staff member per day. Although from what I can deduce, people leave for different reasons; some can't stand the conditions (who would of thought paradise was unbearable), some are removed for breaching the rules, (in which they are endless) and some actually find themselves and what they're looking for, like an intensive therapy and are ready to return to the real world.

I bounce out of my hut and onto the warm sand, no need for shoes on the walk to work through the sandy paths, lush trees and solid timber boardwalks.

A new boat load of staff is arriving today, therefore there has been an air of excitement and whispers passing throughout the island as the staff huddle together to talk about new team members. Each division holds high hopes that for just a little while – they will have a full functioning team. Those bored, and looking for anything stimulating to take the monotony out of the day will take bets on how long each new team member will last. It is some sick game that has been going as long as the island staff can remember.

After my first three weeks on the island, I was informed that a large number of employees lost money betting on me. I laughed proudly at hearing that, yet I was also proud that I'd taken my first step to changing and becoming stronger.

I was expected to leave within the twenty-four to seventy-two-hour bracket at the most. They judged; place of origin, work experience and uniform size request and then placed their bet – no one won that bet, however they all would have, should someone had heard my desperate pleas to let me leave on the very first day.

Clothing size is a strange factor to consider when making a bet, but I've seen firsthand the effects this place has; size sixteen girls on arrival are now size eight with muscles that would rival your average football player. The heat is relentless, the work is punishing and there is no respite. To top off 'island paradise' the staff food is often barely edible, and the lure of the staff bar is much more appealing than lining up to the guest restaurant, waiting to find out, on the incredibly rare chance, that there is actually a spare table once all the guests are seated.

I make a routine stop as I pass the staff cafeteria on my way to work. It is about a two-minute walk from my island hut as I stop to inspect the daily offerings – overcooked bacon, hard eggs and stale bread. I can't say I'm surprised as the past thirty days seem to be like 'Groundhog Day' in the kitchen, so I opt for my usual large pineapple juice and fill my water bottle from the drinking fountain.

No staff appear to be up yet as I wander the empty eatery alone. I seem to have this bizarre early morning rise here which is incredibly surprising to me. Before I left home, I could barely even function before one p.m. in the afternoon; my mind was endlessly lost, and my body alike a simulation of the walking dead.

"Nothing made me happy before." I recollect. A simple task was painstaking as an unfathomable heaviness consumed me all day, each and every single day.

"It is either; a stronger me shining through or a basic survival instinct kicking in?" I consider that thoughtfully, although I'm not entirely sure right now at this point – should I not rise early, then there will be no breakfast juice, no good work trolleys, and I would probably be left with the worst job list of the island for the entire day. This bothers me, not because I like it here, but just because I know, somewhere hidden deep within me, I deserve better.

My new motto, "I deserve better, I deserve better." I chant to myself as I follow the well-worn, sandy path. I move past the staff briefing area and into the storage bays as I remove the work trolleys to commence re-stacking them for the day, quietly going about my usual morning routine.

"Issy, my girl. Good to see you sweet cheeks," he slurs as he slaps me on my ass whilst I re-fill todays work trolleys outside the storage bay doors. I turn around ever so slowly, although I already know, with venom in my veins – instantly, which asshole just laid his dirty unwanted hands on me as I bite back, "Don't. Ever. Call. Me. That. Trey. Back off."

"Ease up their tiger, just trying to be friendly," he replies, winking at me and blowing it off as he saunters past me and into the office.

I'm so angry, I am about to boil over and combust when Katani arrives and leans in close. "Don't let him get to you honey, he's a creep with no morals," she whispers.

"I know." I reply quietly and sigh deep in my heart as my anger dissipates and dissolves into sadness. "I'm so incredibly tired of being treated like playdoh that can be handed around, twisted and thrown away when their finished playing with my heart, my soul and my emotions," I think with an incredible weight of unhappiness within myself.

Meet Trey Maddox – island resident asshole and rooms supervisor. He's been here for about one year, longer than most and has a steady girlfriend in the same sector as me. Sadly, she's completely oblivious to his creepy, inappropriate touching and sly comments to anything that walks and has breasts.

Our department manager, Remington (who we all generally just refer to as Remy) slides right off the other end of the scale, he's totally gay and proud of it but not at all happy I surmise. He would never dare lay a hand, or eyes upon the females in the team, or island for that matter, but instead uses his words and often lashes out at the team for the slightest infraction.

He looks sad and appears lonely most days, perhaps his frustration is easy to vent on a harmless group of girls rather than himself. He is responsible for placing himself on a secluded island which appears to bring him no happiness. "I have zero sympathy to offer him, although I also have no right to judge or assume I understand him," I think silently as I stare at him while he studies the latest work list whilst chewing on the end of his red pen.

Remy mutters to himself, cursing and mumbling about staff levels and new training plans while he runs his hand through his thinning red hair. When a staff member resigns, that particular staff member is required to train the new incoming recruit. It is a great plan in theory, however majority of the staff pack up and leave instantly from the helipad or next boat out. Therefore, there is not a quick enough turnaround time to train a new recruit and often the new applications are less than the islands resignations and departures.

I know all of this as the Human Resources Manager, Scarlett, has a slight fancy for the drink after work and seems to find the nearest sympathetic ear to vent all of her troubles to.

Unfortunately for me, more often than not – that sympathetic ear happens to be me as I'm sitting alone at the island restaurant bar. I make my way to the guest island bar some nights after work. I read or simply listen to the waves crash up against the mass of reef rocks beneath the decking. It's a beautiful view, absolutely breathtaking and simply lends the opportunity for all of my own problems to float away on the wind, out towards the deepest depths of the ocean – even if it is only for a few brief moments, with each crest of the waves.

The issue is, I should just have a flashing sign stating: "Come talk to me and tell me all your problems." I laugh to myself as sitting alone seems to attract people, not repel them.

"Come on!" Katani interrupts my thoughts with a sense of urgency and a smile, tugging on my arm. "Let's go collect the best equipment before the others arrive."

Katani babbles on about the new maintenance guy and how attractive he is whilst I silently pack my things, nodding and smiling where appropriate until we make our way to the daily briefing. I'm so in tuned with pretending to listen and be excited by everyday normal things, when in reality – I am completely consumed in my own thoughts.

Painful thoughts plague my brain all day, every day and sleep seems to be my only real escape. I have no real distractions here and my 'friends' on the island in my mind feel fake, they don't really know me, the real me.

My work is unsatisfying and ridiculously monotonous, although it is exhausting and physically draining. My body screams a resounding 'no' each day as I wake up and battle the intense heat waves and tension wound deep into my bones.

"Island paradise – is nothing like the staff brochure," I smile wryly to myself as I think of my tired body and dream of a day off. My free days off (which are few and far between), are filled with letters home, brimming with more imaginary excitement and explanations of how much of a wonderful time I am having here in 'utopia'.

"Are you listening, Isabelle?" Remy's voice abruptly wakes me from my thoughts.

"Yes, Remy," I reply brightly, repeating what he has just said. "Honeymooners in the beach bungalow want extra towels and hate sand in the bungalow." I smile at that thought. "Why come to an island if you hate sand?" I laugh internally to myself as Remy makes no acknowledgment of my large satisfied smile, after a perfect relay of information he was sure I missed.

"The family rooms are overbooked and need extra beds first thing and the aircon is broken in the waterfront suites 400 – 420. Upgrades are required and those rooms are to be cleaned and locked down with all check-in suites ready for presentation by two p.m. sharp," I finish precisely as I hear sharp intakes of air. Everyone inhales and holds their breath nervously around me, being on the receiving end of Remy's fury is not something anyone wants to experience twice.

Remy looks up from his trademark clipboard without emotion and stares directly at me. "Good," he states flatly. "What are you waiting for?" he questions, scanning the group as everyone scrambles quick smart to collect their trolleys and head to their first assigned guest suites for the day.

Katani bursts out into an infectious laughter as soon as Remy is out of earshot. "You're one in a million Isabelle, you were somewhere else, lost inside your own thoughts again whilst he was speaking, but you recited the speech word for word!" She exclaims as I smile back at Katani with a small shrug.

Remy has never directly raised his voice at me although he does unsettle me with his uncanny ways. He has been more of a silent observer when it comes to me I have noticed since I arrived on the island; never pushing me more than the rest of the team and respectful enough to not pry. "Why I am always the first one at work, why I don't complain (especially about Trey) and importantly why am I here doing this particular empty job, on a secluded island of all the opportunities I could have?" Perhaps he knows these answers but would never dare to ask or he just simply does not care.

Isabelle

I walk slowly down to the beach via the narrow, sandy path hidden alongside my island hut. It is concealed by the most magnificent lush tropical gardens and tall majestic palms, barely noticeable and peacefully untouched. Unless you know it is there, you would walk right past it and continue on down the normal wider, purpose-built beach pathways. The main beach paths, although immaculately kept, don't have the same special allure; worn out by the quad bikes transporting goods around the island and staff trampling across the normal routes each day throughout the staff estate. The staff housing is so cleverly hidden away in the middle of the island – unbeknownst to all the fortunate holiday makers enjoying the natural beauty the island offers. They are completely oblivious to the small community of huts mingled together centrally on the island, including a staff entertainment venue, bar, shared laundry and bathroom facilities.

My days off are generally filled with washing a monotony of the same beachy themed work attire in the shared industrial laundry facilities, (praying one of the machines actually works), then my attempts at photography, (which currently could be described as utterly incompetent, although an A+ for effort), letters to my family filled with beautiful, yet imaginary thoughts (that everyone else wants to hear), and my silent pain working its way at a steady and relentless pace to the surface.

I reach the end of the unblemished beach path, careful not to leave an imprint. I appreciate its simplicity and beauty each and every time I walk this hidden track to sit down on a secluded part of the island.

It is about three p.m. Saturday. With the island walking distance all the way around, it is always surprising when I take this track from my island hut to the beach – no staff or guests seem to ever be here. I feel the wind rushing wildly through my hair, and salty ocean spray captivating my senses as I step out into the open. "It feels as though the elements are embracing me, and welcoming me into their beach home." I consider this with a genuine smile and sense of peace.

I like to think it is deserted because this truly special place has been reserved especially for me, but I know that in reality people are likely too lazy to take the beach paths all the way around from the guest suites to here. There is also an incredible lack of sights on this side of the island according to the long-term stayers, but I would wholeheartedly disagree.

"This is actually my favourite place on the island," I breathe, as I dip my toes into the warm sand and pull out my writing pad from my satchel. I need to work on a part of the 'Isabelle Mission'; check my savings (afford the journey home), review my latest pictures on my camera and write my letters home.

With no phone service, no television, and no internet – I have to write. "I am happy with writing," I consider. "Words are incredibly powerful tools yet; they don't communicate the pain in my expression, they don't allow the visual images of the scars on my body to be seen, and writing makes it easier to pretend I am exceptionally happy to the people I love."

Everything becomes uncomplicated without a face.

I pull my worn hessian bag over my shoulders and place it on my lap as I sit unceremoniously on the sand and set out my beach blanket beside me. I take a deep breath as I pull out this week's letters, postcards and packages. I place them beside me, neatly arranged on my colourful blanket and pull out a drink from my bag.

I decide to open the drink first; a can of Jack Daniels finest Tennessee Whiskey delivered all the way from the mainland to smooth my nerves. I always open my letters in private and I always need to be prepared. My emotions are still raw and I wouldn't dare risk opening them in front of anyone here on the island.

Masking my sadness is a difficult trait, even more difficult when people are overjoyed and read their letters out loud to the captive audience at the afternoon briefings, feeling warmed by the love and affection being sent to them. I miss those feelings as I don't feel them anymore. I feel alone. I feel pain, loss, sadness and a deep, heavy weight resting upon my soul.

I carefully open the first parcel from my parents.

Dear Isabelle,

A few things for you, take care of yourself,

With Love Mum and Dad, xoxo.

"Always straight to the point, their love has never faltered for me, but let's be honest – I am a train wreck on a bad day and completely and utterly lost on any other day," I think sadly to myself. "They shouldn't have to deal with my mess," I sigh, cementing in my delicate mind another reason why I'm here. "People should not feel burdened by me." I decide firmly.

When I reflect upon the 'Isabelle Mission', I still have the daunting; 'decide your next steps' (not on track), blatantly obvious issue. "I guess 'deciding not be utterly and completely lost and finding your own journey' could potentially be the next step?" I contemplate this, scribbling it into my notepad and then removing the contents from my neatly wrapped parcel.

The package contains; new memory cards for my camera, a few new tops, just the ones I like, new socks, my shoes I requested, toiletry items and a few pictures of life at home. I smile broadly as the thoughtfulness overwhelms me and I blink back my silent tears.

The next few postcards are from a few different friends, very similar words in each, although each one brings a genuine smile to my face.

Hey beautiful,

We miss you, hot new club opened! Can't wait to dance with you!

Come home soon babe x

The words turn blurry and I put down the postcards and take another sip of my drink. I will stick them onto my wall beside my bed as soon as I return to my island hut. I have started a little collection of photos and postcards which brings me a smile every night as I climb into bed, feeling a little less lonely with the words and images beside me as I sleep.

The next envelope, I stare at for what seems like an eternity before I open it. I recognise the hand writing and return address. "You can do this" I encourage myself.

It's from him – Elijah Masters.

The sole person who broke me into a million different pieces, effortlessly and single handedly turning my entire world upside down. Alienating me from everything I ever knew and loved, reducing me to a shell of my former self and instilling a feeling within me, less than worthy of life itself, without uttering a single word – that is Elijah.

People say actions speak louder than words. I'm a firm believer in this saying, now and forever after my devastating realisation – without genuine action to support words, the meaning disintegrates. We can say words, articulate meanings to express powerful emotions and feelings, but it is all completely worthless – if all they are is empty words.

"Why does he bother?" I think, angry that he's even decided to pay for a stamp to send this letter. I laugh bitterly to myself, remembering how months ago I would have opened this letter the very second it hit the mail box, sat on the lawn instantly and treasured this very moment as a shining light. A hope everything was a vividly awful nightmare, and my life would be placed back together – fitting perfectly in place, just like Lego's. Everything would be as planned and perfect as I had impossibly dreamed.

I am painfully aware now, this is not possible.

I need to remain strong and be stronger. "You deserve better," I chant over and over as I slide my fingers under the triangle flap to open the envelope and slowly pull out the letter.

Dear Issy,

I hope you read this letter.

I wanted to tell you, I miss you beautiful girl.

I'm so sorry for everything, I wanted to explain this to you in person but you're so far away right now.

I'm incredibly sorry for all the pain I have caused you, you are the most kind and beautiful...

A silent tear escapes me, sliding down my face and dripping onto the page as it turns into a deep painful sob.

I slowly turn over to the second page. I am unsure why I even do this as I feel like I am trapped in a horror movie – one where you don't want to watch but you have to know how it ends.

Without finishing the first page, as the words are cloudy from my tears, I am unable to focus on the second page, no matter how hard I attempt to bring it into a lucid centre. My head is pounding as I make the emotional decision in that moment to tear the pages in half, then in half again and again, until it is unrecognisable and unreadable.

"Asshole," I whisper. There is no one around but even if there was, I simply don't care as I continue to rip the pages up into tiny irrelevant pieces.

"That's not enough," I fume as I pull out a tiny box of matches and make a pile of the torn pieces of paper. I light them up in front of me, my own personal miniature bonfire on the beach, burning away the words meant for me.

"I don't care what they say, nothing can fix this," I admit as I watch the pages burn without regret.

"Words that are too late. Words now burning in the ashes. Words I have set free to float away with the wind." I smile as I release the remaining shredded pages to the breeze, blowing them further and further away from me.

I lay back gently, shuffling my hessian satchel around to use as a pillow, my belongings still strewn haphazardly across my beach blanket as I close my eyes.

Sleep calls to me like an old friend as my body shuts down, protecting me from the pain. I shiver alone as a chill reaches my skin and the sun moves slowly to dip beneath the horizon. It's cold, but I can't move. "I will just rest here for a little while," I think, as I drift off into a beautiful escape and the darkness encases me like a blanket.

Maverick

"Time to go sunshine," beams the voice harshly through the bars of the cell.

The keys rattle loudly as they unlock the cell door and the officer beckons me to move out from behind the bars of my tiny accommodations. I stand and stride out of the mini prison I snared myself in as I attempt to straighten my shirt slightly, frustrated that my favourite black Creed shirt is dirty. I realise I am also missing the belt to my jeans, further irritating me as it makes walking difficult whilst attempting to hold them at a respectable level.

A plastic bag is placed in my hands with my measly possessions – black wallet, belt and black studded wrist band. I'm thinking how little I am worth as I thread my belt back through the loops in my jeans, uncaring of the instructions being delivered to me.

"It doesn't matter," I think to myself. "Nothing does anymore," I seethe as I finally step outside and into the sunlight. I squint, half heartily expecting someone to be there and I sigh at my own hopelessness.

"Who would be here to meet me?" I laugh at myself. I have abandoned my family, and my friends are all probably too high to realise I am gone, or if they do, "would they even remember my arrest?" I consider dejectedly. My so called 'friends' have likely have taken the stance of – "Let's stay the fuck away from that walking disaster." I shake my head in disgust with the realisation how far I have actually fallen.

Any female companions only seem to be attached to the lure of drugs or satisfying their needs with me. The ones that do stay, longer than I would like – I tend to self-sabotage to the point they look at me with pure hate in their veins.

"Fucking great," I curse as I turn and start walking slowly back towards the only place I know right now.

I'm feeling much more alert, clearer than I have been in quite some time. My head is throbbing in pain, although I attempt to push it away as I focus on the swarms of people heading in all different directions, simply going about their daily life.

I wonder thoughtfully about each and every person; couples jogging across the road, people listening to music, the animated discussions of people talking on their phones with wild hand gestures, as if the people on the other end of the phone can actually see their movements, families walking whilst carefully eyeing their children and shouting "stop at the lights, watch out for those people, careful you don't fall."

"Where is everyone going?" I wonder as my mind processes these thoughts with a fascination.

My head dips sharply and I instantly place my hands over my ears in a futile attempt to placate my brain. My mind feels as though it is being dismantled like a second-hand car.

"Although cars can sometimes yield a number of reusable parts of value – I don't believe I can be recycled." I think sadly as I close my eyes in a hollow attempt to wish away my pain.

No one stops to offer assistance, even though I'm obviously suffering.

Not a single person.

Although, "I wouldn't approach me either," I think

negatively as I focus on my breathing, and eventually the pain recedes enough to glance up and take a deep breath. A brief relief as the raging storm inside me has now passed for a moment... this time.

I continue walking, although not at the pace of the world around me, people gently push past me and I take a deep breath.

"Why is everyone in such a hurry?" I consider, as I continue to deflect and extradite any miserable thoughts, storing them somewhere else entirely in my broken mind.

I cross over the intersection and into the park. My entire world and future universe ceased to exist for me six months ago, therefore, it is difficult to comprehend all these people with a purpose, a vision and at the very least a destination.

As I continue walking down the embankment towards the water, I am suddenly stopped dead in my tracks. I absorb the scene before me on my disorientated walk as I finish hiding my gloomy thoughts in the recesses of my mind.

It is utterly breathtaking I realise as I stare unashamedly at the placid blue lake, gently lapping at the shoreline like a peaceful lullaby. My view is partially obscured, although the beautiful willow trees lining the banks add a sense of grandeur and majesty to the scene.

The grand willows are bending painfully over, their slender long branches almost touching the ground, swaying ever so peacefully towards the water below as they whisper back and forth in the breeze. Lush green grass lines the banks all the way to the water, dotted with timber bench seats strategically placed along the winding sandy pathways.

I've been here countless times before I realise, although I have never stopped to embrace the real magnificence of this place.

"It's untouched and it's real," I contemplate as words race through my head. Words forming that could potentially be lyrics to a song. I frown, freezing the lyrical jumble in my head as I cease walking and gaze across the water, lost in my own thoughts. "What am I missing?" I question myself. "I'm twenty-two years old." I sigh, ideally the world should be a treasure trove to be explored at my age, although I left all the best parts of me behind; my family, my full scholarship – to one of the best music and performing arts universities in the world, and sadly also my heart.

I turn slowly and continue walking along the sandy path at the water's edge. I cannot understand what I am feeling as these thoughts parade through my mind, the weight of this incredible sadness grows heavier with each step of my combat boots.

"I am missing out on my life. I am allowing my life to be stolen from me every minute as I continue to live in my worthless state of being." I scold myself. "I am responsible for the dark shadows that follow me. I am responsible for the emptiness I feel. I am the reason I am painfully alone," I continue as I reflect sadly.

I eventually turn back and reluctantly continue to walk towards to the dump of a place I've called 'home' for so long. My feet scuffing the ground, hands cemented in my jean pockets and eyes downcast as I make a journey I am not wholeheartedly invested in.

I rotate the old-style tarnished front door knob and sharply nudge the well-worn timber door open. It has a colourful leadlight arch in the top of the door alike an old Californian bungalow (although much less welcoming, and a hell of a lot less paint left on this door.)

A rancid smell reaches my nostrils once the door is ajar, it's wafting from inside the house. It is a smell that makes an average person retch at; ammonia and stale smoke.

The remnants of drugs cooking and cigarette smoke breaches the doorway as I enter – pooling near the stained plaster roof and under the top of the timber door frame. "It would appear as desperate to escape this hell hole as I am." I think silently.

The air is stagnant and tainted within this dilapidated house I've just entered, or should I say 'been reunited with', after my most recent arrest for some absurd charges I have no energy to comprehend at this point.

"This is the air I have allowed myself to breathe for far too long," I think resigned as I reflect on the few moments I had down by the lake – one of pristine beauty, breathing fresh air next to the water which has a sense of rawness and untouched beauty illuminating from all parts of it.

"Mav?" a quiet voice interrupts my thoughts, prompting me to look across to the old worn brown couch, it's certainly seen better days and I absolutely won't be going near it considering my clearer mind and the abhorrent feeling radiating from this place.

A bony looking girl peers up at me, she looks like she's dead or close to death in my mind. Her body is lifeless and her skin is so pale, she seems almost translucent. Her eyes are rimmed with dark sunken circles, dilated pupils within as I also notice the scratches on the side of her face. She moves to sit upright and pats the couch next to her and smiles sickly. "Sit with me handsome," she slurs.

I completely ignore her. "She is irrelevant," I determine as I turn away and scan the room. I came here for a sole purpose. "A new objective perhaps, a new direction, or at the very least a new destination." I consider this as I survey the repulsive, dirty and barren room – drug paraphernalia line the coffee table, pictures lie helplessly skewed on their hooks, broken objects and rubbish lie fragmented around the old worn scrappy furniture which is sitting haphazardly on mouldy, torn carpet shreds. I feel disgusted. "I allowed this to be my haven, my escape," I think angrily to myself.

The anger sparks quickly inside of me, deep down into my chest and burns within me like a wildfire. It's something I'm getting accustomed to; a spark turns into a flame and a flame instantly bursts into a raging wildfire. I don't know how else to release my emotions, but the anger takes hold more and more frequently with a deep vengeance each and every passing day.

My eyes dart around, purposefully searching as I move from the lounge to the kitchen. It makes me cough as I enter and I'm forced to cover my mouth and nose with my shirt, pulling it up to my face with my hands.

The smell intensifies as I try to focus but my eyes are stinging, it is relentless and only leaves me more determined never to return here again. As the burning sensation in my eyes continue to hinder my search, a male voice stops me in my tracks. "Mav, is that you?"

Someone grabs my shoulder and attempts to spin me around. This only adds fuel to my endless burning anger as I pivot quickly, grabbing him by the neck and forcing him up hard against the kitchen cabinetry.

I realise who it is as my eyes come into a clearer, yet still painstaking focus. I lower my grip as I attempt to reign in my anger (only slightly) and release him slowly. "Yeah, where's my guitar man?" I ask Blake roughly.

Blake could be considered the long-term resident (caretaker) of this evil house, and all its hopeless occupants who drop in and out when addiction takes hold of them.

Upon first appearances, I observe he is dishevelled, yet that should not fool anyone as he is as ruthless as he is cunning. Blake hides in this ramshackle house, and 'caretaker' is too kinder word – I would more likely compare him to a devil wolf, hidden in disguise as a bedraggled sheep, ready to devour anyone with or without a soul, at no cost to him or his conscience. As long as they can pay, he will unashamedly capitalise on (human) opportunities with every step he takes.

Blake raises his eyebrow as he moves around me and props himself up on the opposite kitchen bench. "How would I know man? Chill, sit down and have some candy. Relax brother, where have you been anyways?" He replies lazily, unaffected by our encounter.

'Candy', the inaptly named codeword for drugs in his world and most local haunts if you frequent them enough. You would of had to be born yesterday to not understand the code even if you're not a user, some halfwit must have imagined in all their genius ramblings, that it would be a perfect disguise for adults to be offering candy to one another. Candy doesn't make your mind numb to reality and journey into a land of false possibilities. Nor urge you with an evil hand to make questionable, dangerous decisions and miss days on end in an oblivion that only ends badly. That is indeed what drugs do, manipulating your mind and body – taking away your choices (and conscious ability to make them).

I know I am nothing but another dollar sign to Blake. He has no real concern for my well-being or sudden departure other than his selfish need to continue his dangerous and unhealthy lifestyle.

"I've been in jail asshole, now where's my guitar?" Anger

pierces my voice as I speak.

"Mav, calm down man. What the fuck do you mean you've been in jail? Are we busted? Did you spill? I know they tore the place apart but didn't know they got you," he spurts out. "Bullshit," I fume in my head as I push past him to the hallway.

Blake has little eyes and ears everywhere, so I know he knew exactly where I was and did fuck all other than cover his own ass. I hear Blake slide off the kitchen bench and onto his feet, he follows me whilst I continue to open the doors of the bedrooms in the hallway forcefully, purposefully searching.

Blake follows me at a safe distance behind, he is a lot shorter than me and extremely unfit with the body of a dying twig, and I am blessed with years of boxing experience which makes him a teeny-tiny obstacle in my search should he choose to become violent. Although I already knew when I walked in that violence is not his style (nor forte), manipulation is – in its finest form, and I am in no mood for mind games.

I finally lay my scorched eyes upon my precious guitar case in the corner of the back bedroom. My black leather jacket lay neatly across the top, although from a distance the guitar case seems splayed open unnaturally. I swiftly move closer and open the case fully to see my distinctive black acoustic guitar inside. I sigh of both relief and sadness concurrently, a relief to see my soul in the shape of my guitar, yet a sense of pain and sadness engulfs my entire body, shaking me to my core as I examine the damaged guitar.

"I need to breathe, just breathe and focus on that," I shudder in my own thoughts as I take deep breaths and run my fingers along the beautifully broken strings. This guitar is my only lifeline right now and it is crushing me to see it damaged like this.

Besides the broken strings, my guitar appears otherwise undamaged, although if I knew which fucker did this – I would rip their arms off. The volcano of anger inside me rises to the surface again and I know I need to leave before I do something that cannot be undone. I close the lid of the case over my guitar and clasp the locks tightly without a word. I shift my jacket on roughly over my well-worn t-shirt as I look up at Blake. "I'm out." Those are my last and only words as I walk out of that house with my guitar and a few meagre belongings in a messenger bag – attempting to begin a new verse of my life.

Isabelle

"Isabelle? Belle, can you hear me? Are you okay? Wake up."
 I'm tired and cold. I tense as someone places their hand on my shoulder. I sit up, instantly alert and quickly turn as the hand releases me. I exhale quickly as I realise I was holding my breath at the thought of someone touching me.
 "Flynn, you scared me." I breathe, shivering as I turn back to face the ocean and wrap my arms around my knees and bring them close to me, clinging to them tightly like a safety net of protection. "I am sorry Isabelle, I thought something had happened to you. I walked down here and found you lying here. What was I supposed to think?" he muses as he moves to sit slowly beside me on the sand.
 "Don't worry about it," I reply softly. "Why are you down here?" I ask. I shift to collect my belongings and stuff them in my messenger bag as he reaches to help, glancing at the papers and notebooks strewn around me. "I just come down here sometimes to think, it's a lot quieter than living with Benson," he laughs. "Nearly as good as your roommate," he adds with a wink and I smile at that thought. "Nearly," I reply dryly.
 Meet Flynn; he is (and potentially always will be, if the world doesn't get the opportunity to dig their venomous claws in) such a kind, ~~very attractive~~, no, actually scrap that – incredibly beautiful, swoon worthy – meltdown type of attractive human that I barrelled right into on my very first day. Although, and most importantly, he is one of the most respectful individuals I have

met in my life since the day I arrived on the island, and literally ran right into him.

In typical 'Isabelle style', with a pile of belongings, (I was unable to carry alone – but tried anyway) attempting to find my hut, (after a long sea journey which entailed much of my time lying flat, attempting to overcome wild seasickness) and still nauseous after the 'welcome briefing', of which I heard nothing and only thought of going home, (obviously not by water) and dreaming of some well needed sleep, (for a few days) here he was – the knight in shining armour.

Flynn carried my things, showed me to my island hut, set me up to deal with the onslaught of my seasickness symptoms and proceeded to educate me on island life, (all of which I was drastically unprepared for).

Surprisingly, as it turned out – Flynn lives next door to my hut with Benson. After our initial collision, (my inability to behave like normal human) combined with his sense of general 'suave', I find myself upon arrival a few days later – smiling for the first time in a long time. I listen to them passionately debate whether eggs are best cooked outdoors as they listen to 'Linkin Park'. I sit in my outdoor patio with a genuine smile on my face at the ease and yet ridiculousness of their conversation.

Those two are always untroubled. Often outside cooking on their small portable burner as the fierce sun hides behind the horizon and the breeze sweeps in, they have the music playing whilst drinking cold beers, and usually finish the evening lazing contently in their hammocks. The life style suits them more than most with their laid-back attitudes, warm smiles and crazy antics to pass the time in the low season.

"Come on," Flynn indicates as he stands and pulls my hands

up towards him. I'm eventually standing face to face with him as he pulls me closer and leans down to my ear. "I will make you something to eat," he whispers gently.

Flynn pulls away slowly to see my reaction with a heart stopping smirk, one that would have the entire female island population dropping their panties in an instant.

"Oh, no thanks," I stutter. "I'm okay, I'm just going to head to the showers and then do my washing." I look down at the sand nervously before he can reply.

I'm not good with social skills these days (well that's an understatement) – I'm an entire walking disaster with people, and the very thought of being around other people makes me anxious just thinking about it.

"Well, you're looking skinnier than the usual island population princess. It's Saturday night and I'm not going to poison you – so you will come for dinner on the cook top or I will send Benson over to drag you out." He stands his ground, not letting me past as he places his hands on his hips.

I laugh out loud at his stance. Flynn appears quite strong, muscles peep through his tight shirt and his arms are covered with intricate tattoos I observe as I slowly pull my face back up to his. "No chance of running from this," I think quietly as my brain ticks into overdrive panic madness.

"It's always Saturday night on the Island," I sigh. The only normal thing I can think to say at this point. "But I don't want Benson dragging me anywhere. So yes I will come, but trust me I'm fussy." I smile.

"Good," he says with a wink, turning to head back up towards the island huts. "I love a challenge," he laughs as he marches confidently through the sand and back towards the hidden sandy path.

I stare at Flynn's back as he's pulling the food out from within the mini fridge and placing it next to the portable cooker. He's the islands most eligible bachelor. "Why on earth did he invite me to dinner," I think to myself. "I am a nobody on the island hierarchy of popularity."

Benson abruptly interrupts my train of insecurity. "Sooo princess, how's life living with the dragon?" He laughs. "Uh I guess it's okay," I reply unsure. This unbelievably sends him into a giggling fit and I'm left bewildered at his reaction.

"My roommate is the island misfit and appears to have zero respect or tolerance for anyone. She treats everyone with an air of distaste and wears this disguise proudly." I consider this quietly to myself as I replay Bensons reaction in my mind.

"We understand each other I guess, it's no problem – she means well," I stammer, attempting to close the topic and pull Benson from his giggling fit. It is unnerving to see a grown male laugh himself into a giggling fit and I feel entirely uncomfortable wondering what his next line of questions will be.

Benson lurches over clutching his stomach still laughing at himself as Flynn turns subtly and raises an eyebrow at me. I feel my face heat, turning ruby red with embarrassment with this line of questioning from Benson and Flynn's gaze resting upon me.

Having so much attention in the form of a conversation has thrown me completely off balance. My social awkwardness has reached an entire new level. I interpret a level of pain and confusion that crosses Flynn's face as I sit silently – rendered speechless and completely forgetting how to converse as adults. I don't know how to decipher Flynn's look, nor respond to Benson's mockery, so I look away and stare aimlessly down at my bare feet as I move them through the sand.

I pray Benson moves on to other topics, things that have nothing to do with me as he slurs again. "Ahh so you're saying you are like the island hussy neighbour – partner in crime?" He laughs as his head tips back. Flynn shifts faster than I have ever seen him move as he grabs Benson by the throat. "Isabelle. Is. Not. A. Hussy," he fumes.

I shift up from my camping chair to standing position quickly. As much as I have a burning desire to run away and escape this situation, I believe I need to intervene here as I squeeze gently between them and push them apart. My arms reach out and push Benson and Flynn slowly away from each other with my hands on their chests.

Flynn tentatively complies and releases Benson as I move my eyes from the ground and turn face Benson first, not trusting to move my hands from either of them at this time. With Benson being the most unpredictable of the two in my observations, I look up at him and capture his gaze for a moment before I speak. "Benson, I am nothing like her, but I truly understand pain and loss. People deal with it in the best way they can." I take a deep breath and look away as a thousand painful memories flood my mind. I leave Benson with those thoughts for a moment as I turn my attention towards Flynn.

"You need to back down. Please," I plead with him. My voice is calm and steady as I finish and shift my gaze to look at him directly, (something I am rarely able to do with anyone) so I find I surprise myself with my inner strength in this moment.

Meet Brooklyn; my island hut mate (particular roommate/dragon in question), she is entirely misunderstood and hurting – but I see her, and I see her pain. I feel her pain in different ways.

From what I understand, no one has ever stood up for her, or stayed with her for that matter and I feel obligated to set the record straight, be the voice for her when hers is gone.

No one should face life's challenges alone, and we certainly shouldn't stand for it, (in Bensons case, his disrespect) nor is it fair for anyone to pass judgement on others whom is not standing in their shoes.

Silence fills the air for what seems like an eternity.

Benson stares at me then looks over my head to Flynn. "Uhh I've got to go anyways man. I'm going to see Hanna from the bar shift – she always makes the best cocktails after work so I will catch ya later."

"I am sorry Isabelle," Benson elaborates as he looks down at me and bends to place a kiss on my cheek. He sounds remorseful as he glances from me and then back towards Flynn.

"See ya round," he drawls, whipping his trademark smile back into place as he backs off and spins to leave.

He's hurting now too. I overstepped the invisible boundary between him and Flynn, and he looks ashamed of his actions. "Why can't I do anything right?" I ponder sadly to myself.

Flynn backed away in silence after a gentle squeeze of my hand and proceeded to make dinner as planned, without a single word of what just occurred with Benson. Dinner was also provided in silence, I think perhaps Flynn knew I needed valuable time and space to make sense of what had just happened, with such a gigantic social interaction for me I replay it over and over again in my fragile mind.

Chicken breast, salad and boiled eggs are served on small blue metal camping plates in Flynn's outdoor area. As we sit quietly under the warm sky and experience the ocean breeze, I am actually feeling like I have been magically whisked away to a little food heaven in this moment. I have not eaten a decent meal since my arrival here on the island and it is working hard to distract me from my messy thoughts. Although I attempt to be polite and well-mannered, at the pace I'm eating – it would have anyone confused, 'It's unladylike' as my mum would say, but in this moment I honestly could not care even if I was dining with royalty. The food is amazingly delicious, with tender chicken slices, crisp salad and perfectly soft-boiled eggs.

Flynn works for the island restaurant and the perks are good via the food and supplies he receives to cook on his portable cooker. All other island staff use communal facilities such as the cafeteria, where all meals are served buffet style, the shared barbeque in the staff recreation area, and communal bathrooms – in which the standards are less than desirable.

Although, if I am being really honest, that is not why I'm here eating this meal with Flynn. I am here because I feel overwhelmingly obligated at the gesture, the invitation and my social awkwardness didn't allow me enough time to make up a reasonable, socially acceptable excuse not to have dinner here.

My mind ticks into overdrive thinking about Flynn's overreaction to Benson. "Why would anyone stand up for me?" I consider this as I devour my salad, "I am entirely not worthy of his attention and now I am completely confused." I understand Flynn's high moral compass, although his reaction was so sharp, it took me by surprise. I feel my emotions bubbling away under the surface as I consider Flynn's selfless acts and effortless kindness he offers freely to everyone.

"I consider myself incredibly lucky to have met Flynn. I think the universe is perhaps trying to tell me that not everyone is going to hurt me." I reflect. "I feel the solid stone wall I built around myself cracking just a tiny little bit." I think about this quietly to myself as my emotions reach the surface a silent tear streams down my face.

Flynn moves slowly over to my camping chair. I watch his bare feet move towards me in the sand as my head stays down, fork suspended mid-air as I grapple with my emotions.

Flynn takes my plate and places it gently on the small outdoor table and offers his hand as he pulls me up off the chair. He guides me silently towards the hammock as I wipe my eyes, incredibly embarrassed at the situation I have gotten myself into.

"Hop in," he gently states and points towards the hammock. I look up at him, silent tears streaming down my face. "I'm not going to hurt you, Isabelle," he whispers as he pulls down the hammock for me to lie in.

I climb up into the soft mesh. "Why am I crying in front of the most attractive man on the island?" I laugh to myself. "Only you, Isabelle, would do that," I think as I climb in the beautiful handwoven hammock. I am angry at myself for letting my guard down, but I am in no frame of mind to decipher what that means right now as I struggle to keep my tears at bay.

"So, I have just got Twilight from the mainland, a good chick flick with Edward Cullen." He laughs as he places his palm on my cheek and wipes my tears. "Just what the Island ordered for you." He smiles.

Flynn climbs in the hammock beside me, fires up his laptop and starts working his magic to put the movie on. I don't care what movie it is in that moment, it just feels so peaceful to be swaying in between the high palm trees, under the moonlight and be held by Flynn as he wraps a protective arm around me, with the other carefully instructing the laptop.

"The thought of human interaction is a very terrifying and daunting notion after everything I've been through," I contemplate this as my internal battle rages. I realise sombrely through my jumbled thoughts how much I actually avoid all forms of human interaction, perhaps it was an unconscious decision initially, however the more I examine this, I know that it is becoming intentional to avoid people and ensure I am well and truly alone in the world. I exert effort to strengthen the walls I built around myself every day. I intentionally work hard to lock everyone out of the fortress, these walls are impenetrable. Or so I firmly believed they were, until Flynn. The realisation hits me that Flynn and his shining armour, have ever so slowly placed tiny cracks in the fortress walls, even more alarmingly – is that I feel completely safe right now with Flynn.

"Isabelle, can I ask you something?" Flynn interrupts my internal ramblings as he whispers into my ear.

I freeze instantly. It is almost certain when a person asks: "Can I ask you something?" It is going to be something you entirely do not want to answer. "Sure, depends what it is," I reply completely unsure, anxious of what possible question Flynn needs to ask.

After a few minutes of prolonged silence, Flynn leans closer and breathes, "Why did you hurt yourself Isabelle?"

My heart starts to race unnaturally, as a million memories barrel down on me in that moment. My hands start trembling and I struggle to take a deep breath as I feel the weight of my thoughts firmly pressing down onto my chest. The answers Flynn thinks he needs is not something I can give. "I can't breathe Flynn," I whisper.

I panic with the very notion of not being able to breathe and I struggle harder to take a breath. I feel more helpless and weaker than ever before as the weight of the universe crushes down on me. I don't know if I am hysterical literally or it is all in my complicated mind. I clutch my chest and concentrate on attempting to get air back in my body, I slow my breathing and push back the nausea rising to the surface.

Everything fades slowly to black surrounding me.

I struggle to focus and my ears are ringing so loudly I cannot hear anything. The pain grabs me fiercely and forces me to close my eyes and lay back into the soft weave of the hammock.

I feel my entire body immobilise and I know this feeling well. I slowly succumb to the darkness and gently push Flynn's hand away. "Please don't move me. Please just leave me here for a moment." I whisper, knowing that there is nothing he can do now. I close my eyes and focus on the motion of the hammock swaying me gently in the breeze.

I'm engulfed by sadness as the memories I locked firmly away, all rushed out like an enthusiastic luau; creating quite an impressive display followed by a fire dance in my brain – all unlocked by a few simple words from Flynn. I try to re-gain control of my body, I take deep long breathes in sync with the gentle sway of the hammock, until I finally succumb to a deep sleep, waiting for the dawn to rise for another Sunday in 'hell'.

Maverick

I wander back to the park for a few hours.

I tune out to the rest of the world, listening to my favourite songs on my beats headphones as I lay on the lush well-manicured lawn. My head rests on my satchel, eyes closed, embracing the calmness I feel right now. I have no sense of time or urgency and I feel completely content in this moment.

I breathe a sigh of relief and relish the freedom.

I have no idea how many hours I have been lying here. I only feel the desire to get up off the lawn when a chill reaches my skin, making me shiver. I pull my hoodie from my bag and place it over my head, pulling it down and smoothing out the creases before heading down the path towards the main road in the dark.

Only a few lights illuminate the street as I step slowly down the concrete path. "I need to leave here," I silently and confidently decide. Within that instant, there is a dramatic shift in my train of meaningless thoughts as they are interrupted by the strong, and overwhelming desire to escape.

I've never felt more alive than I do right now. It is as though a person filled with 'hope' has overtaken my broken body and is urging me to do something. "Anything. Be. Free," it whispers as I walk faster now with a sense of determination, although a yet unknown purpose.

I head for the local train station, although I am not entirely sure if it would be open at this time of night. The moon is high in the starlit night and all of today's people on their journeys have long since left, clearing the well-worn paths from the usual onslaught of traffic, likely gone home to be with their families and friends – enjoying life's moments together. "As it should be," I sigh, feeling incredibly alone with that thought.

My determination to leave has me holding a hope that my new journey starts tonight. "It has too," I sigh helplessly. "I can't stay here," I murmur to myself, praying to no one that the station is open when I arrive.

I reach the station, and consider how it feels much grander than it actually is as I peer up at the large columns which grace the entranceway. They are a faded marine blue and white colour, although peeling from years of exposure to the harsh effects of nature.

It is only around nine p.m. and the terminal is still gushing with people shuffling about their daily life, commuting to somewhere. "Every person here has a sense of purpose and direction," I think as I stand and watch people enter and exit the station for a moment.

I walk through the deteriorating station entrance and stare up at the arrivals and departures board. "Where to?" I smile to myself, happy to be free in this moment.

I release myself soundlessly from the self-built prison I have been living in – even if, my liberation will only be for a short while.

I slowly approach the ticket counter.

The young woman behind the desk vaguely glances up at me through the stained-glass panels as I move quietly closer to the window. The glass is hazy from years of neglect and it reminds me of the murky, dirty mirror I peered into not so long ago, as I stood alone in my cell.

"Can I?" She stops mid-sentence.

The attendant looks up and pauses as I stride even closer to the ticket window, actually noticing me now. She gives me her full attention as I approach. I simply raise my eyebrow at her with a devious smile, making her blush from the interaction.

"Can I help you sir?" she splutters, voice shaky as she finishes her question. I would bet she is imagining my body underneath this oversized hoodie.

"I would take her to anyplace, pleasure her until she can't remember her own name, and mine is the only one on her lips, if I wasn't heading out of town," I think deviously.

I smirk at her, knowing I can ooze sex appeal when I'm not displaying my typical 'Fuck-You-World' attitude. "I would like one ticket on the next train or bus anywhere." I smile.

"Uhh, okay honey, let me see what I can do to help you," she replies as she looks swiftly down at her keyboard. She takes her time as she looks at me discreetly, indecisively glancing between me and the computer screen blinking brightly in front of her.

I know she feels my dark eyes boring straight down at her as she attempts to focus on her job and clicks away at the worn keyboard. She flicks her short blonde hair to the side and chews on the end of her pen. "A nervous habit I would assume, as I am positive, no man finds chewing the end of a pen attractive – in a world filled with germs on every surface." I shudder at the thought as she interrupts my silent observation of her.

"Okay, the next train is leaving in about forty-five minutes to the border," she announces.

"It's a long journey, but comfortable," she adds.

"I'll take it," I reply swiftly.

The border; a place I have not entirely travelled before, and although not as exciting as I initially imagined my journey would be, it would be worth it – I hope.

"The further I head north, the warmer the weather, and it's a beautiful part of the country, most of which I have not seen, and apparently, it has an untouched magnificence to it the further you explore." I reminisce, as I replay childhood stories from my parents in my head. On the cold winter nights, drinking cocoa in front of the fire, they would pull us close under a warm crochet blanket, and smile as they told us tales of their travels – the wonderous sights, incredible smells, amazing people and wild adventures they found in all corners of the globe.

"Seems that fate has decided," I think as the attendant shifts nervously in her seat. I look around the terminal while she continues to type on her computer, agitating me with each extra key stroke she takes to print my ticket.

Pain shoots through my head, sharp and intense, barrelling from my eyes to the core of my brain as I wince in pain. "Are you okay?" the attendant asks. She notices my change in demeanour and looks at me alarmed. "Fine. Is the ticket ready?" I urge, pinching the bridge of my nose between my eyes to relieve the pain.

I board the regional train thirty minutes later, taking a seat in the rear carriage at the back, closest to the window. The train is not full, so there is enough room for everyone to be spaced apart with a little bit of privacy. The trains are fully equipped with food service, fully serviced bathrooms and luxury plush seating – enough to keep people happy during long hauls, and I am incredibly thankful in this moment. "It is the most comfortable I have been in a long time," I think gratefully. I slink into the lush seat as I scoot my bag and guitar underneath the space between my feet, smiling with the anticipation of my imminent journey ahead.

I slowly unwind as the train signals loudly, indicating our departure with a shrill whistle as the carriages jolt into motion, slowly rolling over the tracks with a deep thud as the locomotive gathers' momentum.

I find myself remembering my love of the constant rattle and hum as the train races over the tracks, it's such a calming sensation that resonates through my whole body. The journey into the night will be incredibly long, so before I shower I make the difficult decision to pull out my phone, turning it on after months of ignoring it and its incessant demands. The screen illuminates as I take a deep breath not knowing what to expect. It brightens the dark area I'm seated in as I turn the phone to silent mode, seconds before it starts vibrating wildly. The stored incoming messages and voice mails appear on the screen, begging for my attention.

Mum: Seventeen messages. Five missed calls.
Arizona: One text message.
Dad: Four voicemails.

I decide to only open my sister's text:

Mav, Embrace life. I love you. x

"Typical of Arizona," I think, as I genuinely smile for the first time in a very long time. "She's a free spirit, always embracing every opportunity life has given her, and even creates her own wild and bold opportunities." I smile.

She's nothing like me, but we've always had an incredibly close bond growing up. Arizona is three years older than me and currently backpacking around the world with her trio of friends.

I smile at that thought as I'm flooded with happy memories of us. "I remember growing up with Arizona and wouldn't change a single thing." I laugh softly to myself, reflecting on our energetic – yet reckless childhood antics. She was a strong, determined and ever so bossy child. I would have to follow her around (willingly) while she barked orders at me on how to make our tree house. I was only ten years old, attempting to drag the ply wood and materials from the garage to the biggest tree in the yard, with Arizona – standing hands on hips, as a thirteen-year-old project manager, assessing how we were going to build this tree house.

Correction: How I was going to build the tree house for her.

At thirteen years old, it was obvious she was going to be an entrepreneur, leader of her own universe, and that just what she's doing now – thirteen years later. My smile fades and I glance out the window. I miss her fiercely but it's too late to turn back now. I have hurt too many people and it is far too late, I need to do this on my own. I need to free my family from the pain I have caused and the fucked-up chaos that is me.

I turn the phone back off, watching it power down and proceed to take a long hot shower in the one of the allotted sleeper cars. The hot water, change of clothes and peace for a few brief moments worked miracles for my tired body. I make my back through the train carriages and slowly recline down in my plush seat, resting my feet across the empty seat directly in front of me. I place my headphones over my ears and turn the music up, letting the sounds of Everclear radiate through my whole body as I drift off, completely at peace for a moment.

Maverick

My body is woken by the shudder of the train coming to a halt. I glance up as everyone is shuffling slowly in an orderly line towards the front of the train and exit doors. I pull my headphones down around my neck, gather my backpack and guitar, and also head towards the front of the train. I march down the train steps, following the platform and transiting crowd into the border terminal.

I breathe in deeply, embracing the smells around me. The air is crisp and dawn is still hours away as I peer into the sharp blackness that lingers outside the terminal.

"Hey man, where you playing?" I hear. "Huh?" I answer and turn to face the dreadlocked man standing beside me. He smells like weed and beer, and in that moment – I wish I hadn't turned around. The guitar is like a magnet for everyone.

"You play don't you? or you just carry that thing for the chicks?" He laughs at his own joke. "Yeah I play," I reply, "but not for anyone, I just play."

The man looks up at me, I'm quite a bit taller than him I notice as he responds. "That's a dam shame man; music should be heard and felt by everyone."

"Deep." I smile.

"Where you heading anyways?" he asks

"I don't know." I sigh. "Anywhere." He stares at me as if what I said is not socially acceptable and shakes his head. "Take it easy man," dreadlocks states as he turns and wanders off into the dark.

I slowly walk back into the terminal as I consider my next steps. A long-distance train ride to the border has not changed my life and this doesn't feel like it should be the end destination. "This doesn't feel like where I should be, although I did not expect a flashing sign either stating: 'Welcome Maverick, this is the right spot'." I chuckle to myself at the absurdity of my thoughts as I stride over to the departures board, seeking information on my new destination.

All services are finished for the night. "Could be worse," I shrug as I peer around to the hard, uninviting waiting benches. The solid timber benches beckon me closer in my tired mind. I feel as though they are smirking at me, knowing I need to spend the long restless night in the terminal, awaiting the morning departures.

I slump down into the long timber bench and pull out my guitar. It's still broken which continues to infuriate me. All I want to do is feel the strings between my fingers and play – play my guitar until the world completely fades away.

Music takes me far away from all of my agony. It leads me selflessly to another level, a sacred place within my soul. The sounds and the rhythm, is all there is in this special place – everything else fades away to black. Everything is entirely less important in that moment when I play; the music consumes me, and for a single moment – everything in my universe is right again.

"So fucking typical," I fume. Anger pulsing through my veins as I stare at the fallen strings attached to my guitar. "Broken, just like me."

Isabelle

I slowly open my heavy and swollen eyes. I pull my hands up to my face, gently touching the swelling underneath my eyes from a night of endless crying – wallowing in my own self-pity. "Ohh holy shit," I groan as I pull the crisp linen sheet over my head, recalling last night's disastrous events. I'm so embarrassed I want to crawl underneath the hut and never come out. Walking. Island. God. invites me to dinner and I humiliate myself. "Jesus Isabelle, you really know how to create a steaming pile of shit out of your life." I laugh to myself.

I roll over and peer out from under my sheet at my roommate's bed, empty and unmade. "Brooklyn is not home, which should make today a little easier as I don't think I can handle one hundred questions from her today." I sigh with relief.

"Knock. Knock. Sunshine." I hear, followed by feet padding across the front porch. Flynn strolls in the open-door moments later with a huge smile on his face.

No one closes their doors on the island in the staff quarters. No guests ever tread this far inland, and the island staff don't care to intrude on others. The island is far too hot year-round for closed doors, so it's like high school camping for adults – but with no zippers on the flaps at the front of the tents.

Now I'm wishing I didn't follow that trend.

"Oh. My. God," I whisper from underneath the sheets. I think I just died from embarrassment, not only did I humiliate myself last night, but Flynn is now standing in my tiny room –

right next to my bed.

"Please be a bad dream, a really bad dream," I chant in my head. A million different thoughts race through my mind and I hopelessly pray, wishing Flynn's presence in my room was simply a figment of my imagination.

"Ohh come on Isabelle, girls leave my place crying all the time – I'm a real heart breaker you know?" He smiles as he tugs the sheet away from my face and I glare at his perfect set of teeth.

"Not funny Flynn." I state dryly.

"Sorry Isabelle, I'm not here to stress you out. I want to help you," he soothes. "Flynn flashes his 'Prince Charming' smile, cementing in my mind that he believes I'm a damsel in distress." I contemplate this as I sit up slowly.

I smile up at Flynn as I shuffle to reach my feet out of the bed and onto the sandy floor, carefully considering my response as I walk over to the chest of drawers.

I hastily select a pair of denim shorts and a t-shirt from the top drawer as Flynn sits down lazily on my bed. "Look Flynn, I don't need your help or anyone's help. I'm okay really." I reply confidently as I turn back towards the bed to face him.

A wide grin covers his face, I follow his eyes down and notice he is unashamedly staring at my bed shorts. "Ice creams, cute hey?" he mocks. I look down and feel my face flush vivid scarlet as I turn back towards the drawers. "Dammit, today is certainly not my day." I cringe internally. "My far too small, faded ice-cream shorts have been a bed favourite of mine for as long I can remember, not really enticing lingerie or even close to attractive; I think I just died twice this morning." I seethe at my ridiculous stupidity in my head, it is laughable how inept I am at basic, normal human activities.

"Well." I turn back to face him as the blush fades from my

face, hands on hips. "At least the island staff will have something to gossip about for a very long time. 'Me and my ice-cream shorts,' and 'you, leaving my room in the early hours of Sunday morning.' I can hear the whispers already," I smile weakly. "Ughh, people can be so ignorant sometimes." I blurt out.

"Sorry, that just came out." I laugh nervously. Flynn stands up and walks towards me, his face stern, his brilliant blue eyes staring deep down into mine as he grabs my arms softly. "Isabelle, I don't care what people think," He pauses.

"Belle, I want to give you the money you need to fly home. I know you need about eighteen hundred dollars which will take you… say… years," he laughs softly, "to save working here on these wages," he finishes sadly.

I am breathless and stare back at him while I quietly absorb this new information. My thoughts however, regardless of Flynn's generosity – are crystal clear on this.

"Flynn, I don't need your money, I am not a charity case. Yes, I'm a little (excessively) defective and do absurd things, but I don't need saving by anyone, you don't even know me Flynn." I pause and take a breath. "Look, I got myself here and I will get myself out." My voice is calm as I know deep inside me, this is wholeheartedly true. I made this significant promise to myself on day number two of landing here in 'hell' and I've never told anyone before this moment.

"How do you know anyway? Did you rifle through my things while I was comatose?" I continue.

Flynn laughs. "Well not exactly, when I helped you pick up your papers on the beach last night, I seen your savings plan and did the math in my head." He crosses his arms and smiles, seemingly proud of his sneaky calculations and proposal he's put forward.

"Please Belle, I want to give you the money. I've never thought of anything I've ever wanted to do more than this," he pleads. I take a deep breath and linger on the sweet thought of what he is offering before I reply.

Flynn truly is a unique human and the epitome of kindness – but my mind is firmly made up on this one. It is the right choice when I reply contently, "Flynn, thank you. Truly thank you for everything you are offering to me, but I honestly don't want your money. I need to do this for myself."

He smiles gently and nods as if understanding.

I really don't know if he understands the real meaning behind 'why' I need to do it for myself although he continues, "Okay, well the offer stands for the next three months." He smirks with his unabashed charm. "I'm off," he states as he moves in and kisses me on my forehead. "I'm here if you need anything Belle, anything at all," he whispers in my ear.

"Let the gossip mill begin," he laughs as he marches out the door and down the front steps.

Isabelle

The next few months pass by uneventfully, I keep to myself every day in my own routine after the 'Flynn Meltdown' as I refer to it now. I feel myself becoming stronger; mentally and physically, but I'm here in 'Hell Island' where I don't let anyone get close enough to really test the boundaries of the new me.

I attend a few staff functions each week at the insistence of the girls I work with, but I generally keep to myself and always find the perfect moment to sneak off – back to the seclusion of my hut. Flynn still cooks me dinners and sits at the blissfully, uninhabited beach with me every now and then, but I have mentally decided not to let anyone in, so our conversation always ends up being the 'would you rather?' quiz conversation, playing cards or rummaging through the lost and found together. We hunt for treasures in the lost and found such as books and boardgames, long since forgotten by their owners to entertain us and slowly pass the summer days away. He respects my seclusion and I respect him even more for respecting my privacy, and for holding his tongue every time he looks thoughtfully at me, like he is bursting at the seams to ask me more questions.

Flynn has been a solid friend and constant support to me when I tried my hardest to escape the world. I would push everyone as hard as I possibly could away from me, although Flynn was like an unmovable pillar – he simply would not budge. I remember announcing to him during a warm, starlight night on the beach, that he was alike the ocean waves – constantly pushing against the shipwreck caught just out past the reef on the island, (me obviously being the shipwreck in this metaphor) and he simply replied, "no beautiful, actually I am the anchor," with a wink, "just in case you decide to float away."

Flynn and his unwavering support is unsurprisingly even there for me on my last days on the island, the day I stand up for myself, make the right decisions for once and start my new journey (all of which was not part of the 'Isabelle Mission', but the universe has an interesting way of pushing you exactly in the direction you need to go).

"Hey Isabelle! Wait up!" Katani shouts chasing me down the cafeteria steps this morning.

I am still feeling a little under the weather, (understatement; I am barely functioning) so I'm not interested in a larger than life chat, but I turn around and smile politely. "Hey Katani, how are you?" I reply quietly, smiling at the thought of her excessive, high-speed chase out of the cafeteria after me.

"Oh, hell honey, what happened to you? You look like absolute crap," she states as she investigates my puffy face, swollen nose and dark shadows under my eyes.

"I think I have the flu." I roll my eyes, knowing that you have to be close to dying or missing a crucial limb to pull a sick day here.

"Oh, come on Bells, I will make you some herbal tea and help you with your workload today." She offers thoughtfully.

"Thanks Katani, that's really lovely of you." I smile weakly.

We fill our work trolleys whilst Katani talks animatedly, chatting about her new 'island man crush' as she describes him, who arrived last week for the maintenance division. Katani continues on, and I can't help but I smile at her enthusiasm as she launches into a new topic without taking a breath.

Our excitement quickly sours, turning to anger as we spot Trey sauntering into the briefing area. We finish packing and slowly make our way over to the assigned daily briefing point as Katani fumes, quietly venting a long tirade about Trey; how he is constantly giving her hard time everyday about her work standards, and how he won't keep his hands to himself – being the usual sleazebag he is.

My daily round is exceptionally hard today, I've got the beach suites and family rooms. They are overly large rooms with extra beds, mostly situated on the upper levels of the resort. And, as we don't have the convenience of lifts here on the island, everything has to be physically carted up and down the stairs every day. "You know your day will even more hellish when your work board contains the upper levels." I sigh.

Katani peers over at my work board during the morning briefing, it indicates my daily room allocations and her eyes open wide in response. "Don't worry Isabelle, soon as I'm done, I will help you. We all will," she whispers whilst Remy is still talking.

I skip morning break that morning. I'm far too slow when I am sick to maintain the normal workload so I don't allow myself the privilege of a break. I continue to solider on and work through lunch too, sweat pouring from my head and down my back with the intense heat sweltering today across the island – nicely coupled with my raging fever.

I wring out my hessian shorts and colourful shirt as best I can before I enter the last beach suite and turn on the air conditioner. I lean over the end of the bed, placing my hands on the end of the bed frame to brace myself as I take some deep breaths. "I don't know if I can go on today," I sigh helplessly to myself.

I hear the lock mechanism whirr for an instant as the door to the beach suite opens quietly, surprising me. It is very unusual for a guest to enter, or any other staff for that matter during our rounds, the guests are almost always at island activities during the day, and the supervisors only enter once we indicate the room is ready for inspection. I jump up as Trey saunters in with his greasy red hair and dirty face, carrying his usual standard walkie talkie and clipboard. "Hi Princess, what's up? Your very slow today?" He stares directly at my breasts during his opening sentence.

"Leave me alone Trey, I am not well today." I sigh deflated. He laughs and drops some generic pain medication on the bed in front of me. "Someone must have told him I am unwell," I consider as I stare at the medication. "You'll be fine, sharpen up sweet cheeks, I've got guests waiting." He smirks as he slaps me on my ass and turns to leave.

At that exact moment his unwanted hand touches me once again, something fiercely snaps within me. Feelings of anger, pain, and disgust fill me instantly as I reflect upon every unwanted, and inappropriate touch he believes he is entitled to – not just from me alone, but all of the females on the island.

I have never personally witnessed this behaviour with any other staff on the island, but I have heard a number of complaints from Katani and her friendship circles – all of them incriminating Trey, and his inappropriate advances. "I cannot comprehend how he thinks it is okay to behave like a wild animal, and treat people with zero respect," I fume in my head. I slowly straighten up and prepare to face him, stopping him dead in his exit tracks with one word: "Trey."

Trey turns back towards me and I look him straight in the eyes, feeling fire in my veins as the anger pulses through me.

"Don't you ever fucking touch me again. Don't you even dare, lay a single, dirty hand on me – ever again," I state firmly. I'm so tired of being swallowed up by the evil parts of the world, attempting to tune out all the bad shit that happens, brushing it off like a piece of lint stuck to the surface. I know I deserve better in life, and I certainly don't need a sleazebag with no morals touching me without my permission.

The silence fills the room as he stares at me for an endless moment. "He's probably in shock at my sudden outburst," I consider. "A break from my usual nonchalant, quiet and obedient behaviour."

I banish my self-conscious thoughts as I continue, fired up now with a renewed fury and confidence coursing through me. "And, If. You. Ever. Touch. Any. of the other girls on this island, even a look in their direction, or attempt a high five; I swear to god – I will make your life a living hell," I state furiously.

I am deadly serious at this point. I am beyond angry and I am so fired up, so tired of being walked over. I will no longer allow myself to be sexually harassed, nor let the other girls on the island face the same torment. Allowing them to be continuously harassed by the staff supervisor, who has gotten away with it for far too long – grinds against every moral fibre of my being.

Another minute passes in silence, he stares at me and I stare at him. My entire body is shaking as he finally turns and leaves the beach suite – without saying a single word.

I watch him leave as I stand motionless.

The anger and the fight slowly vacates my body, departing quietly as I slump down onto my knees, landing on the cold, hard tiles beneath me. As the anger slowly recedes, it drains the energy out of my body with each ebb, leaving behind a profound sadness that embeds itself deep within my soul.

I am shaking uncontrollably and my tears are flowing slowly down my face, whether it be a moment of relief from what I have just achieved, or the fear of knowing that tomorrow – my life will undoubtably change. I can't stop the anguish I am feeling as I slowly lay my body gently down onto the floor, resting my head softly on the cold, harsh and unforgiving tiles.

I don't know how long I stay paralysed like this.

Seconds. Minutes. Hours. I cannot comprehend time or grasp onto any of my jumbled thoughts as they race past in my mind. It is almost like a slide show in my brain, although it is apparent that within this hectic, internal presentation; someone has pressed fast forward, even though I can see the images appear as they flicker past – they are moving at a speed I cannot fathom.

I wake slowly and feel hands carefully wrapping themselves around me. Voices are murmuring nearby, everything is unclear and distorted. My mind is murky, like wading through a swamp, and no matter how hard I attempt to concentrate – I cannot figure out what the voices are saying. I frustratingly cannot capture a single word as I feel myself being pulled under an emotional tidal wave. I feel myself moving now, I'm being carried and alarm bells chime through my head. I panic, feeling entirely vulnerable as warm powerful arms surround me.

I squirm around, this is a situation I entirely do not want to be in as I try to regain focus. "Shh Isabelle, it's me Flynn. I'm here now, it's okay, I'm here. I've got you baby girl," he breathes in my ear as I close my eyes with relief.

I let the rapids pull me back under as I drift along with the current; knowing I am safe, whilst the endless tears stream down my face.

Maverick

"Mister? Hey Miisster" a tiny voice speaks in my ear as I feel a light tugging on my jumper. "Please Mister, wake up?" the tiny voice pleads as I slowly open my eyes and see a little boy standing incredibly close to my face, smiling.

"Hi" I reply, smiling back at the tiny face in front of me. The boy looks about five or six years old, blond wavy hair and a small round face. I stretch my arms above my head and slowly pull myself up. My neck is painfully sore from using the solid timber arm rest as a pillow for the night.

"Can you play me a song pleeease, Mister?" the tiny voice asks. The boy's big blue eyes grow wider with excitement as he points at my guitar case leaning on the bench beside me. Rubbing my neck and stretching my back, I bend over a little to face the boy. "I'm sorry buddy, my guitar is broken," I reply. The little boy's excitement turns to sadness and his smile is gone in an instant. The boy bows his head with disappointment, he quietly stares sadly at his feet whilst he shuffles one of them in a small circle on the linoleum floor.

"Where's your mum?" I ask. The boy turns towards the ticket counter and points. "Well okay then." I smile. "Let's go find her," I say as cheerily as possible whilst slinging my messenger bag over my shoulder and picking up my guitar.

As I move towards the arrivals and departures board, the small boy speaks. "Where's your Mummy?" Innocent enough question, but it slams me right in the stomach. I hold my breath and feel like I've been winded. All of the air has been knocked out of me with the harsh reality of those three words. "Just breathe Maverick, god damn breathe," I chant in my head.

"EJ! EJ, come here." A woman interrupts the new train of painful thoughts entering my head as I see a woman barrelling towards us with two bags and tickets in her hands. She appears stressed and exhausted as she shouts again in exasperation.

"EJ! How many times have I told you to not to disappear." She scolds him as the boy looks down at his shoes again. "I'm sorry if EJ was bothering you?" She winces. "He's never really listened to the 'stranger danger' talk which makes me crazy." She nervously laughs. "Oh no, not at all." I smile, flashing my brilliant teeth at her. She blushes in response and looks down to my guitar.

"So, are you going to the Lakes Music Festival this weekend?" she asks as an attempt to shift the conversation and mask her embarrassment.

I glance up to the arrivals and departures board, doing a quick scan of the destinations available today.

As I think through my options the woman interrupts my haphazard future planning, "I'm sorry, it's really none of my business anyway," she states.

"Oh, it's no problem," I smile. "Yes, I am going that way," I state confidently. I've just made another unmethodical decision, although I am proud of myself. "Far north coast – sounds perfect," I think to myself, satisfied with my hasty decision.

"Oh, that's nice, sorry again if EJ was bothering you, have a safe trip." The woman interrupts my chain of thoughts as she grabs EJ's hand and turns towards the departure hall, not truly understanding the important moment in my life she has just shared with me.

"Bye EJ," I call out as the boy is lead away by his mother, he turns and waves to me with big grin on his tiny face.

Thirty minutes later I board another high-speed train destined for the north coast. It's almost a seven-hour trip but I am excited, it is an emotion I have not felt in an incredibly long time and it's a breath of fresh air. I feel like a little kid on Christmas day, the feeling of the Christmas presents and the thrill not knowing what is so delicately wrapped inside the glorious paper. I am enlivened with the thought of not knowing what gift I may unearth on my journey north, and equally relieved to experience an emotion other than pure anger.

Most people, I assume would be lonely travelling seven hours alone, even hesitate before making the decision perhaps, heading to another place where they will still be completely alone, but I am incredibly at peace being alone, and so content with my decision and journey to the coast.

Four hours pass swiftly. I feel the train slow and grind to a halt at a scheduled stop, arriving at Lake Arrow for a quick rest break for all the weary passengers. I slide across the seat and out into the isle to make my way to the front of the train. I step out into the bright sunshine and stretch my long legs and arms, twisting my back to release some of the tension wound deep into my muscles.

As I shift my focus, the scene before me is utterly captivating. A vast, placid blue lake laps gently against the shoreline and I find myself compelled to move closer. People bustle about enjoying the stop, knowing the rest break will be brief, but I feel no sense of urgency as I take it in slowly. I appreciate the beauty of this natural wonder as I stroll down the grassy embankment to the water, my combat boots softly crunching across the abundant lawn.

I find a grand, beautiful old maple tree to sit up against as I pull out my notebook from my satchel. The scene inspires me to attempt a few potential lyrics, scribbling them down onto the crisp, yet empty pages. "Now this is free." I smile to myself as I breathe in the fresh air and feel content right now, incredibly happy with the decision I made to leave my self-built prison.

It is the rare moments like these, when the pain subsides, and my anger recedes – that I only wish Arizona was here with me.

I pull my phone out of my messenger bag and turn it on. Again, it vibrates wildly with the incoming texts and voicemails which have gone unanswered for so long. I ignore all of the demands in my world; wanting and pleading through my phone. I open the camera application, focus carefully and take a picture of the lake and its majestic surrounds. I hit the forward icon, smiling as I select the image I have just captured – sending it to Arizona with a brief message:

For you Arizona, embracing life. Love Mav. x

I turn my phone back off and feel happy that no matter how far away from Arizona I am – I know the eternal bond between us is unbreakable. I can feel her spirit thousands of miles away.

Maverick

This coastal town is everything I dreamed of – music spilling out of clubs and restaurants at every street, culture and history oozing from every building and the long timers always ready to tell a story, their passion overflowing out of them with every new story they share.

Their passion and zest for life is inspiring. I try to embrace opportunities that come my way as my raging feelings of anger start to dissolve ever so slowly; all the hate and pain start to drift away as I find peace and solace in my music as the months pass by.

I met an incredibly kind, old soulful man upon my arrival that irrevocably changed me. Deep down, slowly and patiently, without my knowledge and despite my hot-headed protests at every turn – he changed my heart and soul piece by piece. Much like rearranging a puzzle, he gently clicked the pieces back into place where they belong.

He brought all of my emotions back to the surface, even when I had them buried so deeply. I buried my emotions in a vault, hidden underneath all the fierce and burning embers within me, but he gently pulled and pulled through the toughest of fibres, and patiently battled against all my wrath and fury.

Every time I crumbled under the weight of it all – he was always there to navigate me, hoist the main sails and weather the most tempestuous waters, right there alongside me – each and every time I fractured like a turbulent storm.

It was the first night I arrived when I met Walter and I only had one thing on my mind – fixing my pride and joy – my precious black acoustic guitar. I received directions from the information centre at the train terminal to the heart of the town, and to the guitar shop where I could buy the strings I needed to repair my guitar.

An unseasonal thunderstorm had fallen during my walk to the store, so as I opened the shop door, I felt a sense of relief to no longer be pounded with relentless rain, but I was angry. Very fucking angry; angry with the bells that jingled as I walked in, angry it was raining and angry that everything in the world seemed to be against me – even the god damn weather. My moods were as unpredictable and as wild as the ocean, I could instantaneously go from calm and peaceful to a giant angry swell very quickly. I felt as if the tide was pulling me under and I was helpless to stop the crushing feeling that overtook me with every breath. I was drowning and resisting against the urge to fracture something with each new wave of fury.

"Can I help you, young man?" the old man asks as he peers up at me over his glasses, not letting go of the instrument he's working on. "Yeah," I reply gruffly as I attempt to shake out my jacket and peel off my wet t-shirt. "I need to fix my guitar," I state bluntly as I pull a fresh t-shirt out of my bag. I remove the old one and shove the new one over my head, smoothing it down while I await his response. My voice was neither kind nor polite, I am angry, my head is pounding and I am frustrated without any real cause. I'm like a ticking time bomb waiting to finally explode.

"Well let me see what I can do, take a seat and let's have look at your guitar." The man was indifferent to me as he replied and gestured towards the stool in front of the counter he was perched at. I pull out my guitar and place it carefully on top of the bench. "I see," murmurs the old man. "We'll have this fixed in no time for you," he smiles. "She's a beauty." He beams as he runs his fingers along the body of the guitar.

I wait, thrumming my fingers on the bench for what feels like entirely too long in my abrasive mind whilst he works meticulously on my guitar, perched at the bench on the opposite side of counter. Even though I have no destination after this one, my patience is a very thin piece of twine – ready to snap with the slightest draft as I feel my anger slowing simmering away and ready to boil for no valid reason.

Finally, the shop owner slowly shuffles towards me and hands me my guitar with a huge smile on his face. I feel slightly less agitated and a sense of relief washes through me as I adjust to sit on the stool – one leg on the ground and the other perched on the peg with the guitar resting on my thigh. I tune the guitar and strum lightly, letting the hypnotic sounds fill the room.

"Will you play me something son?" the shop owner interrupts. "Will I?" I think to myself. I'm craving to completely lose myself in the music, forget everything, even for a just a single moment, but I am entirely unsure as I play for me, my soul and my emotions – not the captive audience. "Although, it is only one old man," I consider, not Wembley Stadium.

"Uh sure," I reply hesitantly after a few moments silence with my soul crying out a resounding 'Yes!' and my mind thrumming an unmistakable 'No' deep inside my head. "What do you want to hear?" I ask as I slowly peer up at him and then back down to the beautifully new laid strings on my guitar.

"Whatever is in your heart," replies the old man softly.

I think for a few seconds and start strumming the guitar, playing the rift that initially comes to mind. 'Wish You Were Here' by Incubus. I start softly, my voice low as I sing with everything I am. I close my eyes and feel the sounds as I drift into my own world of melody. Through the verses and chorus I feel myself float away, the music taking me away – far, far away from anywhere.

As I draw to a close, the man smiles gently and rubs his salt-and-pepper beard (more salt than indeed pepper). "That was amazingly beautiful son. I'm Walter," he states as he extends his hand out to shake mine. "Thanks," I reply nervously, shaking the old man's hand. "I'm Maverick, Maverick Black."

"Where are you from Maverick?" Walter asks.

"Not from around here." I sigh as I inspect the old man. He's certainly old in years but his face is defined and chiselled, deep lines etched in his skin and his hair is whiter than I have ever seen. "I see, so do you have somewhere to stay?" enquires Walter.

"Why do you ask?" I reply defensively and the old man chuckles at me in response.

"Son, you walked in here dripping wet, carrying your belongings on your back and you have not checked the time once in the past hour. I am old, but not stupid you know." He smiles and raises his eyebrow at me, waiting for my comeback.

"Oh." I shrug as I pull my messenger bag over my shoulder. "No, I don't have somewhere to stay, I just arrived so I thought I could find a motel in town after I fixed my guitar." I look down and focus on my guitar, anywhere but the man standing in front of me. "I have somewhere you can stay as long as you like; it's just down the road, furnished, warm and dry." He nods slowly and solemnly.

"Oh, thank you." I rush out as I pack my guitar away. "But

that's not necessary. I don't want to intrude on you and your life," I finally blurt out after a few seconds deliberation.

Walter lets out a long hearty laugh. "You're not staying with me Maverick. I have my sons warehouse you can stay at, it has been refurbished and no one lives there anymore." He sighs, his happiness sliding away from him, his features downcast, almost as if he remembers something unimaginably painful within his own memories.

A minute passes in silence as I consider this offer. "That's really generous of you Walter, but why would you offer it to me?" I enquire. "No one gives handouts to anyone these days, and people can be the most selfish creatures on this earth," I think negatively to myself. People are not selfless and the universe is not kind in my mind.

Walter slowly looks around his store, I'm assuming it is whilst he considers his response. As he observes his shop filled with memories, memorabilia and diverse instruments, he eventually turns back towards me and sighs, "Maverick son, throughout our lives we are sent precious souls, meant to share our journey, however brief their stay, they remind us why we are here, no matter how short that stay may be on gods earth."

"That's why you Maverick, that's exactly why," he states solemnly.

Isabelle

"Isabelle? Belle?"

"Wake up beautiful, please baby girl. Come back to me," a soft voice calls to me as I feel a feather light kiss on my forehead.

I feel the shift and dip on my bed as someone sits beside me. "Isabelle? It's me Flynn."

I open one eye very slowly and peer up at him. "Hi Flynn," I reply quietly, yet albeit sheepishly.

"Isabelle. Hi Beautiful Girl." He smiles with his incredible Hollywood style teeth and stunning dimples on full display. "How are you feeling?" Flynn asks softly as he brushes my hair aside.

"I'm okay. Just tired I guess," I reply as he hands me a glass of water and pain killers from beside my bed. I slowly push myself up, raising my back against the pillows and rub my eyes to scan the room. I mentally confirm it's almost dawn outside as I peer through my sheer blue curtains. A profound sense of confusion and loss creeps in as I understand what I am looking at – and the time I have lost.

I peer around to my right and notice although Brooklyn's bed is dishevelled – she is not here once again. This hurts my heart and messes with my fragile emotional state as I ponder where she is, and if she is indeed okay. I feel completely lost without her right now. Although she doesn't say much, nor support me in traditional ways, I do wish she was here for me – knowing she simply gets me. She understands me completely and irrevocably without question.

Brooklyn and I don't communicate on a level that others understand, and as much as we deny it, our own unique experiences painfully and intensely collide each and every day. It is although we swim around the deepest oceans, navigating those cold waters in the dark together, however it is not something we talk deeply about – ever. I understand her, and she understands me, and I need her right now. I need her sitting here (angry as usual) or in any other mood for that matter, as long as she is beside me as a supporter, someone flying my flag and cheering me on as an enthusiastic fan.

I swallow the pain killers from Flynn and gaze out through the sheer curtains again – It's too early for work based on the sunrise and heat so I can only assume Brooklyn is asleep on the beach, or has been enthralled by the new staff, and enticed for a one-night-stand, all of which will certainly not help her or her self-esteem.

"What time is it?" I ask, feeling exhausted. Although in the same bone-tired breath, I feel I have missed a monumental moment, and large portion of my life being asleep.

"You've been asleep for fourteen hours Belle. Do you know what happened yesterday?" Flynn asks quietly as he looks away from me and down to his feet, twisting his hands together anxiously.

"Do you know what happened Flynn?" I urge back in response, apprehensive to know if he understands entirely what happened in the beach suite yesterday with Trey.

The movement catches my eye as I glance down at Flynn rubbing his palms together. "What the hell have you done Flynn?" I cry as I observe his split and bruised knuckles.

"Calm down Isabelle, nothing I shouldn't have done," he proclaims.

"What does that mean?" I scoff upset as I grab his hands and pull them close as if to take his pain away with my touch. "It means I lost it yesterday Isabelle. I could have killed him if it wasn't for Katani," he replies abruptly and angrily as he looks away again.

"Oh Flynn, I'm so terribly sorry," I whisper. My distress turns into a sad longing ache as I hug him from behind, resting my head gently on his back. I inhale Flynn's scent, it's fresh and earthy as I slowly wrap my arms around his waist, hoping to provide some miniscule of comfort for him.

A minute passes, and another as I feel his chest rise and fall as my body moves in sync with his. I cannot fully comprehend why I'm not afraid of Flynn. I'm utterly afraid of every other human in the universe, but everything always feels gentle, safe and kind with him. Something I should entirely be protecting myself from, as generally – it's all treacherous waters, but with Flynn it is absolutely different. I feel unreservedly safe and grounded with him. I feel wholly protected in his presence so I open myself to be vulnerable, and I know he needs me right now. I know that, truly deep down within my soul as I pull him closer and attempt to take his pain away.

"No, I'm sorry Isabelle. I'm truly sorry," he whispers as he turns and kisses my forehead.

I love it when he does that, it makes me feel unique and special as part of his universe, something that is impossibly hard for me to reconcile in my chaotic brain.

He gently grabs my chin, lifting so our eyes meet. "I finished my lunch shift at the guest restaurant yesterday about four pm."

He starts slowly. "I took the guest path back and as I was untying my apron – Katani came barrelling right into me. She looked up at me Belle; her eyes were filled with fear and panic, she was hysterical, screaming over and over at me a jumble of words I could not make sense of. I couldn't grasp what she was saying Belle, nothing made sense." Flynn shakes his head, like the memory is too awful to recall as he slowly moves and grasps my hands between his, rubbing my palms softly.

"I grabbed her arms and shook her gently, enough to get her to centre herself. I had to shout her name over and over until she stopped and could actually focus on me," he continues. "All she said was: 'Isabelle. Help Isabelle please,' she was so panicked I thought you had..." he finishes without finishing that sentence.

I understood completely and feel incredibly grief-stricken in this moment. Flynn cannot finish that sentence as he chokes up, his earlier anger has subsided for a real and powerful pain as it engulfs him. I'm so incredibly lost that I have caused this anguish as a tear rolls down my face, to have impacted Flynn in this way shatters my fragile heart. Flynn forces a smile and slowly wipes my tears away with his hand as he continues, "I started running with Katani back up the beach path, she rapidly explained you were in the furthest suites near the back beaches. I quickened my pace but I didn't know which one you were in, so I had to slow up for Katani to catch up, and open up the suite you were actually in. Fucking ridiculous automatic locking doors." He breathes.

I hold in a tiny smile with Flynn's exasperation, knowing Flynn's feelings on automatic locking doors. Flynn and Benson were accidently locked in the sweltering supply shed for a few too many hours recently. When someone eventually found them, they were glowing with sweat with no aircon in the non-perishable sheds – just two, apparently ineffective ceiling fans.

87

They were completely wasted as it happened to be the one of the sheds storing the islands dry goods; including the alcohol reserves. I hold back my smile at the memory as they stumbled out like an episode of survivor; shirts off, pants rolled up, no shoes, dirty sandy feet and hands, squinting dramatically (and entirely drunk) as they were released back into the world, although, they did have a hell of a lot more supplies on hand whilst trapped in 'captivity'.

Flynn interrupts my delightful internal replay of that moment. "We moved Isabelle, faster than I think I have seen anyone move on this little island. You were…" He can't finish that sentence either. I feel like my heart has been ripped out of my chest with his words, left tattered and beating quietly in his hands as I bring my palms to my face in shock. My tears continue to flow again with the weight beneath the Denmark Strait – as I feel myself reliving the intense anger and pain I felt yesterday.

"I'm so sorry Isabelle," he whispers.

"No Flynn, you have nothing to be sorry for," I state distraught, my voice shaky and barely audible.

"I found you on the floor of the suite shivering and when I tried to get through to you; you were agitated, confused and unresponsive to me Belle, it was almost like a catatonic state." He pauses, "I lost it baby girl. I lashed out and screamed at Katani and for that I am so sorry, but I was so consumed by anger, I didn't know who or what had hurt you." Flynn explains as he grips his knuckles tighter. "Katani explained very quickly – the short version of how she was coming to help you as you missed break, and lunch, and you were sick." He looks at me with a deep heaviness and look of despair, unable to contain his emotions, his eyes rimmed red as he runs his hand through his wild blonde hair.

"When she got to the door, she heard you." Flynn won't even acknowledge his name so I know now he is fully aware of what has happened to a degree. I don't understand the extent of how or why this has impacted him so deeply, but it is a level of care that thoroughly overwhelms me – joining my all-consuming patchwork of thoughts. I move closer to give a gentle squeeze of his hand and let him continue, I don't know what else to do in this moment.

"Katani mentioned he stopped her at the entrance to the suite, preventing her from entering. Apparently he 'needed' to check her daily rooms sheet, and interrogate her as to why she was at your beach suite, instead of cleaning the common areas – where she was supposed to be. That asshole stole precious minutes, delaying her to you, and I am struggling to understand if that was intentional. I honestly don't care right now Belle, for me, if what he did was intentional to delay her; that will only add a whole entire level of fury to my resolve, as I am fighting within myself to deal with all of this." He elaborates as he sweeps his hands around in a circle, indicating us and the room as a unit; a complex mechanism working together to essentially function.

Flynn sighs whilst my mind struggles to process his complex emotions, and attempt to unfold them within mine. I remain deathly silent as he continues the dreadful montage of events – leading to this exact moment in time. "That fucker swept past her once he'd finished his interrogation, without a single word of you." He states with a vigorous anger.

"Katani went to you beautiful, she tried but it was not enough and not quick enough. You were not responding and she was terrified, so she ran to get help," he softens, explaining sadly as he turns to look at me again whilst bringing his hand to cup my cheek gently.

"Is Katani okay?" I ask quietly.

"Isabelle. That's not even a question right now, are you okay?" he replies abruptly.

"I am okay Flynn, please don't worry about me. I just couldn't take it anymore and I needed to stand up for myself. I just couldn't take it," I repeat softly as I look down at our intertwined hands.

Flynn grabs me and pulls me closer onto his lap. "Isabelle, I'm so sorry, I'm so very sorry," he repeats over and over in my ear. His warm arms wrap around me and I embrace the closeness and protection I feel right now with him. We are quiet, a peaceful yet not uncomfortable silence for what seems like a lifetime. The wind sweeps in my window with a delicate breeze as Flynn holds me close and the sun rises higher into the sky.

"Flynn, can I ask you something?" I whisper into his chest, fighting back against the inner demons relentlessly haunting my mind.

"Sure beautiful, anything?" he asks as he places a gentle kiss through my hair and into the side of my head, landing softly just above my ear.

I take a deep breath, internally mustering the courage to finally ask: "Why do you care so much what happens to me?"

Flynn immediately shifts and pulls me out so I'm facing him. I'm still sitting within his lap, although we now sit eye to eye and I hold my breath, hesitantly awaiting his response.

"God... he is incredibly beautiful. A blessing to mankind with his heart and soul akin to that of an angel, yet I have no idea why he cares, nor why he specifically cares about me." These thoughts plague me relentlessly as I silently observe him. Flynn appears vulnerable in this moment; his blond hair unkempt, his face unshaven, and he looks like he hasn't slept for days, although he is still, without a doubt – the most breathtaking sight – effortlessly capturing my untamed imagination. It is beyond that though, surpassing the beautiful exterior facade of Flynn, underneath lies the most genuine, understanding and generous person I have ever met.

Flynn throws himself at everything as though he wants to leave nothing behind, and inexplicably changes the lives of everyone and anyone he encounters – like no stone will ever be unturned to his sunshine. It is like his heart and soul are always shining; as bright as the sun and more magnificent than the moon itself. There is a gravitational pull towards his positive energy and light that not I, nor anyone who encounters him – can escape his distinctive phenomenon.

I slowly peer down at his solid arms and back up to his face as I observe his unique tattoos, once again they invade my imagination as I inspect them, snaking boldly up his neck and peeking out from underneath his shirt. He waits for my eyes to reach his again. "Isabelle. People care. I care. You're so wrapped up in being angry and independent." He shakes his head in disbelief. "I don't know who hurt you, and if only I knew, I would make it my mission to tear them apart, exactly like they tore you apart beautiful. I want to break them into miniscule pieces, so tiny that it is impossible for them to place themselves back together, nor create a foundation to hurt anyone – ever again." He takes a deep breath and sighs, shifting his gaze from me to the window for a moment. "You fucking deserve better baby girl – but you are the only person who cannot see this." He grinds his teeth and rubs his hand through his hair – his anger bubbling dangerously close to the surface as he continues and I remain completely silent.

"Isabelle, the day I found you at the beach, crying in your sleep, so innocent, so hurt. I vowed to protect you whilst you were here on the island. You triggered something buried so deep inside of me on that day, but I must admit, it started much earlier than that…Your very first day on the island when you barrelled right into me," he smiles. "So fierce and so independent you were; breaking though all of my emotions and obstacles I had tirelessly built. You instantaneously broke me princess with your: 'Fuck.You.World' – I can do this on my own attitude." Flynn laughs refreshingly.

"Although it wasn't until much later when I realised you wouldn't willingly ever accept my help or completely open up; not to me, not to anyone ever. I wanted you to re-gain your strength, independence and your beautiful soul baby girl, therefore, I vowed wholeheartedly and without reservation to protect you whilst you did that for yourself Isabelle." He sighs defeated. "I failed Isabelle. I failed you and I will never forgive myself," he whispers as he shuffles down, placing his head in my lap gently, losing his internal battle and finally succumbing to extreme exhaustion and his own internal conflict.

"Oh Flynn, you didn't fail, you didn't fail at all." I urge, rubbing my hands through his hair as he lays on my lap.

"I won this battle Flynn. I am stronger than before and I made the right decision to stand up to Trey. I know you are there, always for me, every step of the way…" I stumble to place the right words, this seems so intimate and yet my mind cannot catch up with my heart in this moment. "I can't ever repay you Flynn, for your kindness and support. Words won't ever be enough," I whisper, not expressing even one per cent of my feelings.

"My feelings are firmly locked away in a rigid safety deposit box within my heart; a place so secure, much alike the secret archives in the Vatican." I dare not tell Flynn a single word of this as I reflect to myself. I gently rest my forehead against his and move to kiss his cheek gently, lost within my own thoughts.

Katani bounds in the open door of my hut a few minutes later. "Hey team, how's my Isabelle?" she asks cheerily.

"You're in a good mood," I state as I slide gently away from Flynn, back into the safety of my bed and pull the covers up – feeling a little exposed.

"I'm feeling great Isabelle!" She exclaims with excitement. "You won an epic battle for women; all the ladies here on the island, and most importantly you stood up for yourself, I'm so incredibly proud of you Bells. That filthy stain has gone forever," she states, whilst jumping up and down clapping excitedly. "Katani has never held back her direct thoughts, or any thoughts – ever for that matter, her internal filter is never on, although I do love her energy." I think to myself, feeling absolutely exhausted, even after my deep and lengthy sleep.

"What do you mean 'gone forever'?" I question, afraid of the answer regardless. "Should I have pressed Flynn further?" I think disturbingly to myself.

"Well after your—" she stumbles, looking directly at Flynn. Interestingly, and completely out of character for Katani to reign her words in, I am left wondering if Flynn told her to dial back her unshakeable declarations as she continues, "after your message was delivered loud and clear to Trey, he slinked right back to briefing office, immediately spouting as many lies and bullshit ramblings as he could muster to spin this tale, in his favour of course – directly to Remy. Meanwhile and interestingly, Brooklyn was actually home when Flynn and I brought you here, and I thought she might actually explode as soon as she laid eyes on you." Katani smiles at Flynn with an unspoken agreement.

"Her temper is remarkably worse than boy wonder here." She winks and points at Flynn from head to toe. "Anyways, Brooklyn demanded Remington – and an entourage of the island medical support personnel, come immediately to see what happened, and ensure you got the best medical support necessary." She emphasises this dramatically with her hands, as if I was present and alert in the room when this actually occurred.

"Remy seen me like this?" I asked embarrassed, plucking that particular thought out of everything Katani has just told me. "Remy seen all right – he was furious Isabelle. I've never seen him so angry." Katani breathes. "He lost it at Trey. Completely. Lost. It. He marched back to briefing office after the medical support team had seen you, although, it was more like a 'strut' you know, in a Remy kind of way." She laughs.

"Katani…stay on topic." Flynn sighs.

"Right. Yes well after that, Remy called Scarlett from HR down to witness the statements immediately. I relayed my version of events which I heard from the door of the beach suite, followed by Trey… repeating his lies after I had given my statement. He is such a lying asshole." She scoffs, hands on hips, with a stance that looks as though she is modelling the latest fashions on the Milan runways. "Anyway, the rest of the team arrived back to the briefing office at close of shift, hearing his version of bullshit events he 'believed' occurred, and the real kicker – are you ready Isabelle?" she questions, although I don't actually get a chance to respond before she continues with a wink.

"Isabelle, all of the female team had a complaint of a similar nature against him, some worse than others – but they all support yours," she claims. Katani smiles widely, like she has just won a prize for this declaration. "Treys gone Isabelle, he was flown off the island on the helipad; instant dismissal and probably a string of charges against him." This is an incredible amount of information to absorb as I sit in silence for a few moments, navigating what all this means.

I feel overwhelmed as Flynn grabs my hand gently, rubbing his thumbs along my fingers as he slowly turns towards me. "You've got a flight home next week booked by Remy, all expenses paid," he trails off.

"What?" I question in frustration, as I lay my head back on the pillow dramatically with my arms splayed out beside me. Both Katani and Flynn look at each other and then back towards me with bemused expressions.

"You don't want to go home princess?" Flynn asks softly.

"Yes, I do, you know I do very much want to go home." I sigh. "But I wanted to do it for myself. I saved just enough money for the journey last week," I explain with a smile. "My first independent act." I gush with a twirl of my hands for emphasis. If I had of been standing, I might have even attempted a graceful bow and hand twirl like a symphony conductor – elaborating just how incredibly proud I was of this achievement.

"Second Belle, second fiercely independent act," Katani corrects me with a smile.

Isabelle

I'm waiting at the jetty to board the catamaran a week later; starting the journey home to the mainland via the island catamaran, then a bus trip to the airport, and long flight home to the north coast. Everyone is there as my eyes scan the crowd, so many people have skipped work for thirty minutes to see the staff departures and say their goodbyes. This makes my heart swell with pride. "People might actually like me," I think to myself, increasing my self-esteem by a tiny amount as I smile with that notion.

The boat is moored and I can see the island crew ushering the guests onto the boat in an orderly fashion. "Staff will be next to board," I smile as Brooklyn approaches me first. "Hey Roomie... thank you," she starts nervously as she fidgets with her hessian shorts, (if I ever see hessian again – it will be too soon). "You're the only person who ever stayed with me." She genuinely smiles in a rare display of emotion.

"Brooklyn, you need to take care of yourself, you are worth it. Remember that," I encourage in her ear as I hug her close.

Work colleagues and friends from all departments usher past and whisper their goodbyes and well-wishes. Benson grabs me in a tight bear hug, spinning me around awkwardly whilst others move out of the way of his dramatic goodbye. Hanna hands me a little pink cocktail she's brought down to the jetty for a "proper bon-voyage" as she calls it. I sip on the delightful cocktail as I say my own good-byes to those staying on for another season.

Remy is next as I take a deep breath and give him a big smile. "Isabelle! Darling," he exclaims as takes my face in his hands. "I'm sorry. So very sorry, I wish I had of known darling girl. You're an amazing ray of sunshine and I will miss you. Be strong, be kind and stay beautiful." He smiles as he kisses me on my cheeks as if we are in Paris, complete with the "Mwah" for real authenticity.

The words are stuck as my emotions start to bubble up. "Thank you Remy." I smile and try to hold back my tears that are threatening to break out. Remy smiles deeply and moves back down the jetty as I see Katani pushing through the crowd towards me. She is already crying, tears glistening on her face when she reaches me.

"I love you Isabelle, you've shown me true courage and what it means to create inner strength to carry on – no matter how hard things may seem. I miss you already Bells," she sobs in a typical dramatic Katani way.

"Katani, you're beautiful, funny and smart. You can do anything you want in life. Don't waste it here," I breathe. "I will miss you too Katani, so much." I break away from her hug and slowly take her hand. "I will take these happy memories with me always." I smile.

I feel incredibly blessed to have met so many wonderful people on this journey. "These memories and lessons are priceless," I think to myself as I watch Katani leave, wandering slowly back up to the jetty to finish her shift.

I turn slowly back towards the boat and stand frozen to the spot when I catch sight of him, suspended in time as I suddenly notice Flynn standing on the end of the jetty.

A small platform juts out at the furthest end of the jetty where it reaches a lookout point, positioned directly towards the stranded shipwreck in the reef, although, Flynn is leaning over the railing, peering down into the translucent blue waters instead. "I have stood in that spot countless times before." I smile in reflection. "I would stand for hours, watching the colourful schools of fish swimming in a magnificent synchrony, once again lost in my own maze of thoughts." I reminisce as my attention shifts back to Flynn. He looks almost at peace; although my mind is anything but – full of turmoil like the waves crashing against the catamaran moored at the jetty.

I take a deep breath for courage, absolutely not knowing what I'm going to say once I reach him. Flynn has opened my eyes wide to a whole new world of possibilities. He's shown me people do have the capability to be kind, patient, love, protect and care for others, and importantly – he didn't give up, slowly chipping away at my anger against the entire world. He's shown me that perhaps I was mistaken, so wrapped up in my grief that I was wrong. I was so determined that the universe was against me, when in actual fact, once I slowly let go of my pain, I realised – there are good people in the world. People who care, people who are not set on a path of destruction out to hurt others, and people who take the time to shelter others when they need it the most – when they are unable to do it for themselves. Flynn is a brilliant shining light in a dark and chaotic world. I feel as though the universe brought me Flynn as a gift, and Flynn in turn – brought me back to life.

 I muster up a tremendous amount of bravery, walking over to Flynn and leaning over the railing as I stare down at the stunning water next to him. It is a magnificent clear blue at this time of the day, the translucent waters are filled with thousands upon thousands of brilliant tropical fish. It is truly breathtaking as the clear waters rush up against the worn, yet steadfast jetty pillars, and a diverse mecca of marine life dart backwards and forwards beneath our feet.

"You know," he starts in his beautiful deep rich voice, "someone once told me if you love something – let it go, and it will come back to you when the time is right." He shifts to face me as he leans gently against the balustrade.

"Flynn," I whisper, my heart pounding. I am still unsure what are the right words in this moment as he interrupts my internal derailment, a complete train wreck of thoughts as I stand beside him.

"Isabelle, I'm letting you go. You need to be free, carve your own new path beautiful. But I will find you… when the time is right. I will come for you Bells," he states confidently. Flynn envelopes his muscular arms around me, holding me close and ever so tightly within his protective sphere.

"Isabelle, if you need anything, if any fucker hurts you, if you need to talk – remember, I'm always here for you and I will be waiting for you, when you are ready." He slowly peels me away from him as the weight of his words steal my breath away.

I feel him staring down at me, his beautiful soul reaching beyond the facade of me. I cannot look up yet. I cannot look him in the eye whilst I grapple with my emotions, attempting to wrangle my heart back into my chest. "I will find you Isabelle. And I will love you, like you deserve to be loved," he whispers in my ear as he moves closer, gently kissing my cheek. I hug him back fiercely in return, wishing this moment was endless.

"Thank you Flynn." I breathe. "I do not know the right words… right now for you," I start shakily. I pull away slightly from our embrace so I can look him in the eye. "Although, I do know, you are so incredibly special to me Flynn. I hope the universe gives you everything you want in life. You deserve to be happy," I whisper as tears stream down my face.

"Goodbye Flynn." I smile and place a gentle kiss on his cheek before I slowly release him, turning to walk back towards the catamaran for the final boarding call. I join the queue with the departing island staff, giving Flynn a final gaze as he remains unmoving, stoic on the end of the jetty platform.

I smile broadly between my tears as I walk proudly up the gangway and embrace the ocean sounds and smells. I silently whisper my final goodbyes to the island itself that sheltered me from the storm that was me. I feel a little less heavy, unburdened and free – a little more alive as I step onto the catamaran for the very last time.

Maverick

Walter gets me a gig a couple of nights a week singing covers and playing my guitar in a local bar. I'm not the star attraction, but that suits me as I fade into my own world of music when I play. I need to get used to 'playing for a captive audience' as Walter describes it, although I feel like I'm more background music for the drunken revellers who frequent the bars in this town.

I become closer to Walter as the months pass. He's a kind soul and luck perhaps has it, my first night in town he offers me to stay in his son's warehouse – rent free. Walter won't hear it any other way, but the absence of his son plays on my mind night after night. I sit perched at the kitchen island bench, clenching my beer in my hand, twisting the icy cold label off the bottle, and leaving the tiny torn pieces on the bench as Walter approaches me. He moves slowly through the warehouse with a genuine smile as he sits down and joins me for a beer.

Whilst I brace myself to ask him before tonight's gig, I contemplate the reasons why he never talks of his son. "Does my family also not talk about me? Have they moved on? Am I simply a distant memory to them?" I consider these thoughts sadly.

Walter chats happily away about his new instruments, and the people he has met recently in his store, 'on his journey' as he likes to call it. After a few courage beers, I muster the nerve to finally ask curiously, "Walter, where is your son? You never speak about him?"

It's been a troubling thought in my head for months now. He doesn't ever mention him and a thousand possibilities rack my mind day after day. I watch the colours slowly fade from Walter's face after the words leave my mouth as he solemnly stares down at the kitchen bench. All the rosy blush in his cheeks disappear, along with his hearty smile – leaving behind a painful, empty white ghost sitting beside me.

Walter slowly peers up at me after a few moments and rubs his hand through his white hair. "He died two years ago Mav, motorbike accident." He exhales and returns to staring at his beer as he shifts, slightly angling himself towards the decking and the view outside.

I feel like my heart has been ripped out of my chest instantly, and it's impossible to breathe. That is not what I anticipated of all the possibilities; I imagined a strained relationship or distance even, but never considered death. "The loss of a child would be immeasurable," I think sadly at the pain and anguish he has experienced.

"Oh... Walter," I stutter. "I'm so incredibly sorry for your loss. I didn't know," I enunciate slowly with my chest aching. I feel an overwhelming sadness for Walter. No one should ever have to lose their child. To outlive a child, your own child would be the worst imaginable scenario. They have their whole life ahead of them – one you created out of pure love. It is devastating and I cannot fathom the pain he is feeling as I drag my own painful memories to the surface.

An awkward silence descends as I silently curse myself. "Fuck, I always say the wrong thing," I think as I shake my head and wipe my hands on my jeans – afraid to look up at Walter. I despise myself as I consider what I have done to bring these distressing memories back to the surface for him.

I slowly peer up at him. He looks like he's engulfed in pain and I can hear it in voice as he continues. "A drunk driver veered into his lane one night on his way home from a mates place. He died on the scene Mav, he was only twenty-three." He pauses for what seems like an eternity. I place my hand over my mouth and hold back my own emotions; his unexpected death, his life unfairly cut short – all resonating deeply within me. I can hear the old clock ticking over the fire place as we sit together in silence.

"You know Maverick, life is short, embrace every opportunity that comes your way. Love fiercely the people who love you, and make the right choices." The pain etched in Walters's voice hits me hard. I'm rendered speechless as Walter stands and comes to rest his hand on my shoulder, giving it a gentle squeeze. I sit motionless as he leaves slowly, closing the door to the warehouse softly behind him with a gentle click.

My brain ticks into overdrive. I'm hurting now too, and I have no idea what to do as I feel a barrel of emotions hit me with the intensity of a freight train. "What can I do?" I sigh helplessly. I feel once again adrift and lost, furious at life, and agitated as I feel the fires reignite – burning once again deep within my veins.

I hastily pull out my phone from my messenger bag as I move over to the living room. I sink down into the couch, impatiently waiting for the screen to illuminate. The phone vibrates wildly with the stored incoming unread texts. I angrily swipe the notifications away, again without reading them as I hit the phone icon, searching purposefully for the letter M. When I reach the stored number I am looking for, I attempt to compose myself, taking a deep breath, still unsure of my own actions as I anxiously hit call.

"Mav? Honey is that you?" Mum's voice is stretched with concern, and yet a hopeful question lingered at the end of her statement.

"Yeah Mum, it's me," I reply softly as she takes a deep breath and starts sobbing down the phone.

"Oh Maverick, my beautiful boy, where are you? Come home please," she pleads.

I take a deep breath and pinch the bridge of my nose, I'm fighting back my own tears now, and my voice is quivering. "Mum, I just wanted to tell you that I love you." I state it with conviction as she sobs even harder.

"Maverick please, are you okay? Where are you? I will come and get you," she states firmly.

This is devastatingly hard. I place my hand on my head, running it through my wild black hair and sigh. There are not enough words, or at least not the right ones I can think of in this exact moment to alleviate her suffering. No words can express the darkness and chaos that has been me – what I'm feeling, where I've been, or even where I want to be.

"Mum I'm fine. I'm safe… I just need some time. Please Mum don't cry, I'm so incredibly sorry. Just know that I love you, always remember that," I enunciate the latter, feeling my heart break simultaneously with hers.

I hang up quietly and slowly turn my phone back off, staring aimlessly at the screen whilst I attempt to reconcile everything – every fucked-up event that has that has happened to lead me here… to this exact moment.

Isabelle

"Isabelle. Sweetheart!" I wince as my friends Madison and Skylar concurrently shriek down the phone excitedly.

"We are so excited to see you tonight! We will pick you up at eight p.m.," Skylar states quickly.

I have been home for about three weeks now, and avoiding the entire world was not working out as much as I had envisioned. I have reluctantly given in, agreeing to head into town to a local bar for the night with a few friends. Skylar and Madison could not contain their elation when they knew I was returning from the island. It made me smile, brimming with happiness as they enthusiastically made immediate plans to visit me. The effervescent duo would not accept my futile protests against a night out, and have flown in for the weekend, staying at their parent's holiday houses on the coast with me.

Our parents all own beautiful coastal homes, and it is well-deserved with how hard they have worked to achieve their own dreams, building sustainable and unique futures – ones that they truly desired.

Reflecting upon our parent's wealth, "I am happy for their successes, although, it continues to aggravate me when people assume 'money fixes everything', and 'all rich people are happy'." I laugh at that thought as I learnt that lesson painfully. "It is not true at all – money truly cannot 'buy' your happiness. Happiness comes from within ourselves, and it's a treasure far greater than gold." I reflect and smile at the memory of Flynn –

more valuable than any element the earth will uncover in the shape of metal.

I needed another escape route after leaving the island so I found myself here in this beautiful coastal town with a love of music and history, topped with the most breathtaking sights and incredibly passionate people.

"What the hell am I going to wear?" I sigh as I walk from the kitchen up the hallway and into one of the rooms I've moved into while I'm living here.

My parents left today, they flew in when I arrived onto the coast to their holiday house and stayed for three weeks. Mum eagerly cooked all our favourite meals, we laughed wholeheartedly as we reminisced upon past events, played boardgames to pass the days and Dad made his famous cocktails each night as we watched the sunset peacefully from the jetty. Not once did they ask why I was home early or why I flew into their coastal holiday home rather than our actual house, although the question of 'what's next?' lingered precariously in the air.

I told them of my plans one starlight night as we sat out on the jetty enjoying the breeze sweeping in over the lake. I explained my intentions to apply for a few photography jobs here in this vibrant coastal town, genuinely smiling as I declared how photography had piqued my interest whilst on the island.

This was wholeheartedly true, I discovered on the island that I do actually enjoy capturing moments in the form of images. I appreciated the peacefulness to it, surprised with its relaxing nature which calmed my erratic thoughts, and I was becoming quite good at it, (or so I thought as my self-esteem slowly, yet patiently claws its way back to the surface). I have already started building a portfolio to submit to a few local places advertising for work, excited at the prospect of exploring this new adventure.

"I know I am not quite ready for home or university life again just yet, so here on the coast is going to be home for a while." I smile with that thought as I think of my journey at the moment, it is much alike a 'choose your own adventure' book; you get to decide the next steps and where they lead you – blazing your own unique trail.

I finally decide upon my ripped faded denim boyfriend jeans and a tight black corset that belongs to my sister, accessorised with my usual black studded wrist bands to cover the hideous scars and my favourite gold cross around my neck. The large gold cross is attached to a long, chain link necklace. It's not a religious statement, but I like to simply just be me – unique inside and out, driven by my own distinctions, completely irrelevant to others, although significant to me.

The necklace called to me when I found it hidden in a small boutique; of all the gems, crystals and charms, that was the one I felt entirely compelled to own and wear it proudly. I reflect on Flynn's words as I place the chain around my neck: *"Like scars beautiful girl, they are unique and should be worn proudly like a crown – a crown of everything you have overcome to be the person you are today."*

Although I'm still failing miserably at attempting to hide from the entire world, I do believe I am becoming a stronger version of myself. I know I need to make better choices for myself and ultimately just be me – be the very best version of myself I can each and every day. "This should have always been the case, but I now understand that we all get a little lost sometimes on our journey." I consider this carefully as I move to locate my make-up case in the bathroom, rushing to get ready before the girls arrive to collect me – for a night – I'm not entirely sure I am ready for.

The car beeps twice loudly at just past eight p.m. outside my house and I wander out slowly, grasping my handbag like a safety net. I realise, although externally ready, internally I am entirely not keen on going out to the local haunts.

Although this coastal town offers such a diverse mecca of restaurants, bars and entertainment – I am terrified. The thought of so many people in one space, coupled with the uncertainty of it all, has me completely on edge. Although, the stronger version of me, urges me forward with a persistent shove, knowing deep down I don't want to be a total recluse anymore.

"You don't need to hide, you need to embrace life." I chant in my head, feeling Flynn motivating me as he invades my memories. *"Be brave princess, you've got this."* Flynn supports within my mind as if he is right there beside me, whispering in my ear, followed by a gentle squeeze of my hand and kiss on my forehead for encouragement.

Madison is honking the horn and Skylar is hanging out of the passenger window with a drink in her hand. "Hurry up Isabelle, there's a new hot bod in town and not a minute to waste!" she proclaims.

"Oh… Hi to you too Sky," I reply dryly as I open the back door of the car and slide in.

"Chill out babe," replies Skylar. "We are so excited your back and we want to hear all about it!" She claps and jumps up and down enthusiastically in her seat as she reaches behind to grab my hand, giving it a gentle squeeze. I laugh out loud at her exuberant reaction whilst Madison manoeuvres out of the driveway and into the traffic. Madison is entirely focused on navigating, zoned out to the full force of the energy and excitement Skylar is exhibiting.

It genuinely makes me smile at her jubilance to see me.

Skylar's exhilaration is something I was completely not expecting as I continuously wrestle with my hauntingly low self-esteem.

I sigh with a smile, "There's not much to tell Sky, it was just hard work; hot, sticky and endless work really." I stare out the window, reflecting on the island, the hardships I endured and the lessons I learnt.

"Oh, I think there's a lot more to tell than that babe, you look so damn sexy, like a new woman just floated out of that house. I want to know all about it!" she exclaims as she turns back in her seat and smiles at me with a wink.

Madison glances through the rear-view mirror at me and returns a kind smile with her usual trait, a single eyebrow raise that sums it up: 'I know' it says, without saying a single word. We continue to chat about work, my plans for my portfolio and Skylar's studies as we approach the venue, only a very short drive from my house.

"Let's go," Madison interrupts. "We're here." She smiles as she jumps out of the car and straightens her jacket as she quickens her pace to the door.

"What's the rush Madison?" I ask, jogging to catch up with her as I swing my bag over my shoulder.

Before she can answer Skylar yells from behind me: "That... would be Cruize," she shouts as she breaks into laughter at her own bold statement.

I'm intrigued, but I dismiss Skylar and swiftly move closer towards Madison. "Who is Cruize Madison?" I ask as I pull her arm gently, tugging her to a stop before she reaches the door. Madison slowly turns and smiles. "He's just... someone new Isabelle. Someone I met, and I like him," she states as she looks down at her feet, twisting her handbag strap nervously between her fingers.

"You know I'm happy for you right?" I claim as I gently grab her face. Madison slightly pulls away slowly from my embrace, her eyes intentionally avoiding me as she stares nervously at her feet with a look of apprehension.

"What's wrong Madison? You didn't want to tell me, did you? You thought I would…" I trail off as my hands fall away from her. I stare at her and consider how my actions have impacted her in this way. "I have completely fucked-up," I realise silently as Madison slowly looks up at me.

I feel a little bit more internally broken as I comprehend that perhaps I am the cause of her anxiety and sadness. Madison's eyes shimmer with unshed tears as she looks at me and starts. "It's just… you were so heartbroken and… damaged, I didn't know how to tell you." She shrugs, gazing sadly at me, twisting the straps even tighter on her handbag.

I pull her in for a meaningful hug. "I love you Madison, and I am happy for you, so very happy for you," I whisper in her ear. "Don't ever think you should hide your happiness from me, I will always be here for you," I explain. "Now, let's not keep him waiting. I would love to meet the guy who has captured Madison's beautiful heart." I smile genuinely as I release her, tentatively waiting to gauge her reaction.

"Thank you," she breathes with what I assume is a sense of relief. It appears as though the weight of the universe has been lifted off her shoulders as her brilliant smile lights up her whole face. "I missed you so much." She smiles as she grabs my hand and turns back towards the entrance.

"This guy… must be really something special to her," I think happily to myself as we march across the gravel to the entrance.

Skylar rushes forward and pushes the door open with a dramatic hand twirl, inviting us in before she makes a beeline directly to the bar. "What'll it be ladies?" She smiles as she pulls out her credit card and wiggles it in front of us.

"Spoilt rotten," I think playfully as I roll my eyes. Skylar's parents give her everything and anything she ever wants, she's never ever gone without; if you imagine Cher's wardrobe in 'clueless', double it and then double it again. My parents could do the same but we were brought up with a different outlook, and my determination to forge my own path makes me who I am today. I would never take their money and use it as my own personal spending account, unlike Skylar, I prefer to earn and pay for what I need as our parents distilled an appreciation for money in us since we were very young. We were taught that in order to have what you want; you need to work hard, set goals and never give up – everything is achievable. In cohesion with that and my new-found journey I am attempting to create, this brings about such a radiant sense of independence. A sense of satisfaction and achievement which is unlimited; not relying on anyone else but myself to carve my own untravelled path is a sense of profound relief – alike a gentle breeze on a hot summer's night. My parents have never questioned my choices, always supported me in every endeavour (regardless of how unconventional) which I believe makes me the person who I am today. "Leader of my own universe, or pretending to be. I'm not sure which one yet," I think as I prepare myself for the night ahead.

We gather our drinks from the bar and slide into one of the booths filled with generous and lush red couches, collectively selecting a spot near the stage. As we settle in, whom I assume must be Cruize, saunters over and gives Madison a gentle kiss on her cheek, making her blush a vivid shade of scarlet. "Hi, I'm Cruize," he states politely as he extends his hand out to greet me. I place my drink back on the table and stand to formally meet him, shaking his hand with a smile. "You must be Isabelle." He beams back at me with his brilliant smile. "Yep, that's me. It's lovely to meet you Cruize," I reply as I shrink back down into my seat and stare awkwardly at my drink. Cruize moves comfortably into the booth beside Madison and wraps his arm protectively around her as the conversation starts up again.

I scan the area for any sign of anything that would make me anxious. That list is endless so I decided to just focus on my drink – and the time. It is too early to leave so instead I shift my attention back to the conversation as Skylar chats animatedly. Skylar hardly takes a breath as she fills me in on everything and anything she thinks is of importance whilst I've been away. I smile and participate, semi-involved until she interrupts her montage of events and gasps dramatically, bringing her hands to her face excitedly.

"He's here!" she exclaims and claps with exuberance.

"Who?" I ask curiously.

"You'll see soon enough," replies Skylar with a wink. "Something to cure a broken heart," she sighs and clutches her chest like a scene out of Romeo and Juliet.

"Uhh… Skylar my heart is not broken?" I reply quietly.

"My heart is dark and cold, locked so deep inside a vault that no one has the keys to – not even me," I whisper, far too quietly for anyone to hear the latter.

"Whatever," she replies as she flicks her hair and scurries off to the bar to flirt with the local football team who have made their way in. Madison and Cruize cuddle up – entirely oblivious and completely involved in their own blissful new world.

Isabelle

I hear him before I see him.

The most beautiful voice I have ever heard in my life.

I hold my breath and slowly turn around in the booth to face the stage where the mesmerising sound is coming from. He is singing the Goo Goo Dolls: Iris and I feel as though the breath has been slammed out of my body with the force of a hurricane.

I peer across to see him for the very first time; eyes closed, strumming the guitar and singing his entire heart out.

I feel compelled to physically stand now, embracing the music and depth of his words as he sings each line with conviction – his soul laid bare to the audience.

I lean my head back and close my eyes as I attempt to take a deep breath in. This man's incredible voice has stolen my breath away with only a few words, and as much as I would prefer to deny it – I'm entirely entranced by him, his sounds, and this very unexpected experience.

I slowly bring my head down and open my eyes to face him. I listen intently to every word he sings as my heart swells, completely absorbing him, the song, and this extraordinary moment. A meaningful tear escapes my eye and streams down my face, my thoughts heavy as I brush it away without notice – relating to the depth of his words, and feeling more than anyone will ever know.

"Isabelle, dance with me!" Skylar screams in my ear as she pulls my hand, dragging me towards the dance floor as my eyes simultaneously lock with his. He stares directly at me with the weight of a billion stars as he sings the rest of the song. His dark, jet black hair washes over his left eye and I can see his lip ring shimmering within the stage lights. His eyes are dark, and yet mysterious as he gazes directly at me – like we are the only two people in the room. "He is so incredibly beautiful, and... yet different," I think to myself as my mind empties and my heart races – beating only for him and his melody in this very moment.

I struggle to breathe, unconsciously holding my breath whilst attempting to comprehend how surreal this moment feels. "I feel as though we are standing alone, somewhere intensely private; the room devoid, apart from us, his guitar and the lyrics washing over me in tidal waves – as if they were only ever meant for me," I reflect surprisingly to myself.

"Isabelle!" Skylar urges, tugging on my hand and pulling me out from within my internal trance.

"Sorry honey. Let me go to the bar first, then I will dance with you," I reply with an attempted smile as I pull myself away from her. "I need a minute to compose myself," I think confused, unable to process the rampant emotions coursing through me, and appease my menacing mind.

I march towards the bar in my magenta coloured boots, carefully avoiding the mingling bodies in between as they talk animatedly, laugh vivaciously and dance ever so closely together without borders.

I eventually, and gratefully rest up against the bar, leaning on it like a lifeline as I order a whisky, reminiscing on my apparently 'unorthodox behaviour' as I have been told – although I honestly don't care.

"Having a pink frilly drink with an umbrella and a straw is not what I need right now. I need to take the edge off and absorb everything I just unexpectedly felt." I sigh bewildered.

Some of the football jocks saunter over near me at the edge of the bar while I wait for my order. I can smell the grass, dirt and sweat from today's match as they converge. I feel an unwanted and heavy arm lace around my shoulders. "Helloo... Lady Isabelle," he slurs. "Where have you been hiding princess?" He drools in my ear as I comprehend Jake's unwelcome arm – wrapping tightly around me.

The moment he touches me – the anger and memory of Trey rises up, building inside of me like a wildfire. "I entirely don't understand why any person feels it is okay to touch someone without their permission, or at the very least, garner some type of mutual friendship or affection before doing so." I fume internally.

"Not everyone is the same baby girl – trust in that, and trust in me when I say – not everyone is out to hurt you." I inhale sharply, recalling Flynn's words. I utter Flynn's advice silently to myself, attempting to relax my anxious mind as I concurrently inhale Jakes scent; reeking of beer and body odour, mingled with far too much cologne to mask the fact – he most certainly has not showered after the game tonight.

The football team converge into the town year after year, all football season with an air of arrogance and self-entitlement. I have always stayed as far as possible away from them, although, being a small coastal town – everyone knows everyone – and you need to work a hell of a lot harder to live a private life here in this tiny piece of paradise.

I knew, even in high school, spending my breaks here with my family – that I would not allow myself to be treated like a pretty little handbag to be carted around and displayed. From what I have heard, some of these men certainly do not treat women with any form of respect, and the stories that are shared and evolve from every football season are despicable; degrading women and speaking as though they are expendable, along with the attitude that 'their feelings don't matter.' This thought haunts me relentlessly. Women to them are simply accessories to be used, and then discarded once the novelty has worn off.

I hastily pull myself out from under Jake's arm and swing around to face him. "None of your business, Jake," I state confidently as I grab my drink from the bar and make my way back to the safety of the bench seats with Madison.

Madison is still completely engrossed in Cruize when I return to the booth. It pains me a little to watch them, my chest aching with an all too familiar feeling of loneliness. A feeling I have tried so incredibly hard to escape, although I know – I should not feel this way. I did not lie to her, I am so incredibly happy for Madison, but it is extremely hard seeing someone beyond happy, protected, safe and loved in a universe that excludes everyone else – when your own world is a bitter tangled mess.

My thoughts drift back to Flynn as I feel a drastic sense of loss without him I realise. "I miss him immensely," I consider as I sit and stare emptily at my drink and the bar menu. I attempt to avoid looking at anyone, nor drawing attention to myself as I reflect on island lessons 101 – being alone seemed to attract very unwanted attention when I was trying so very hard to repel people and not encourage them. Although, sitting here uncomfortably and solus, I acquire a compounded and renewed, all too familiar feeling of isolation and separation from the rest of the normal functioning world.

I feel constricted, a tightening and uncomfortable feeling in my chest seeps in as I take few deep breaths. I clutch my chest gently and drink faster than normal in an attempt to drown out all the awful memories that are threatening to surface.

"Just breathe Belle, nothing is ever as bad as it seems within your own imagination." I hear Flynn resoundingly through my mind as another memory invades my senses, grounding me just a little bit more as I struggle with my emotions.

I ponder these scrambled thoughts for a while as I drink, friends replacing them one after another while I slink back into a deep, dark abyss once again. My thoughts are muddled and confusing as I try to slow my anxious brain and re-join the world.

"You don't have to be ready yet, take the time you need sweetheart. The universe will wait as long as you need it to." I recall Flynn's advice again during one of our many conversations. It is absurd how I was so determined not to let him in, (nor anyone in fact) although he tried anyways – day after day.

Flynn found ways to slowly scale the fortress, placing tiny cracks in my concrete walls as he patiently guided me, provided understanding without judgement, and stood beside me as I grew stronger a little more with each passing day. It was almost predictive as I feel his presence strongly now, and rely on his advice – echoing through me with every tentative step I take.

The venue is getting rowdy. I glance at the time registering is it almost midnight, I've well and truly had enough as I work through the chaotic internal mess that is me. I feel myself fading and desperately in need of sleep. "I'm going," I state to Madison as I stand and swing my hand bag over my shoulder, wrapping it around my waist like a security blanket.

"Don't go Iz, we won't be much longer." She smiles happily as she nuzzles into Cruize's neck.

"I will see you tomorrow, I've had enough," I reply quietly as I move to kiss her on the cheek, say my goodbyes to Cruize then navigate slowly through the surging crowd towards the front doors.

I don't have a jacket (another ridiculous decision in my murky mind) although it's crisp outside, a warning perhaps of the long winter nights to come. I hug myself for warmth, rubbing my arms as I walk briskly across the car park, starting the journey home.

"Heyyy Isaabellle, whyyy the hurry? We were just getting to know each other better?" Jake slurs worse than the earlier encounter, all too close within my ear as he once again swings his heavy arm around my shoulders. I turn to stop and face him, pulling myself awkwardly out from underneath his arm.

"Jake. What do you want?" I urge as I push him away from me with both hands.

"I thought we could get to know each other?" He smiles and moves closer again so I can smell the beer on his breath and the sweat from his body as it once again assaults me.

"Jake, Jesus, leave me alone. I don't want to get to know you anymore than I already do." My voice is shaky and increasingly louder.

"Leave her alone." A deep voice interrupts.

Jake moves his drunken head to his right to see who's there. "What's it to you?" he slurs. The unknown voice takes another step closer into my view and I gasp with recognition.

"It's you," I breathe.

"She told you to leave her alone; I'm just seeing that you make good with her request," he replies as he leans on his guitar case.

"Hey mate, why don't you fuck off and mind your own

business." Jake spits and moves in an act of aggression, turning to face the singer who captivated my soul inside that bar tonight.

"I wouldn't do that if I were you," the singer states motionless as he stares him down, through his almost jet-black eyes with arrogant stance that beckons: "just try it, if you dare."

I can see his muscles outlined through his black shirt as I observe him more closely. "He looks strong, very strong," I think to myself. "Jake would be slow in his current capacity even though he is a footballer, very slow to react," I consider. "Why am I even thinking about this?" I curse to myself. "These two are not having a fight right here and right now." I acknowledge this to myself, knowing I cannot handle anymore conflict as I step in between them in a rash decision and turn to face Jake. "Jake, go home, you're drunk and going to do something stupid. Think about your football scholarship," I state sharply and push my hands in a futile attempt against his chest away from me and the guitarist.

Jake stumbles slightly in the gravel, although rights himself and moves around me as he leans further to the right so he can once again face the singer over my head. "You're mine pretty boy. You just wait, you're dead." He points at him over my shoulder.

"Don't I know it," the singer replies nonchalantly as he stares directly at him and raises an eyebrow as Jake turns and stumbles back towards the bar.

I storm off towards the main street after the altercation, angry that life has a way of slamming into me like a freight train at precisely the moment you don't need it to. "It's like an avalanche you find yourself ominously stuck under, and then to top it all off, a rock lands directly on top of you after the avalanche to confirm the actual fact – you well and truly are a hazard, a walking disaster that unwillingly invites drama and chaos into your life no matter how many barricades you put up." These thoughts barrel through my head as I hear the mysterious singer jog after me, his combat boots crunching heavily against the gravel pathway.

I walk faster, picking up my pace to escape back to the safety of my self-imposed isolation and protection of my home. "Why did you do that?" I hiss at him as he catches up, still marching down the road and not even turning to face him. "Are you okay?" he asks.

"What do you care?" I snap back and stop abruptly, turning to see his reaction.

"Where are you going?" he asks, completely ignoring my question and creating a perplexity in my mind.

I take the time to inspect him, a large tattoo snakes up his arm reaching all the way to his neck, it's similar to Flynn's although even with a brief inspection I know it has an entirely different meaning – one I am eager to know. He's wearing tight black ripped jeans which fit him perfectly with a matching black t-shirt and studded wrist band. "Matching wrist bands," I consider as he interrupts my silent inspection of him by moving a step closer. He is now standing incredibly close to me and I can smell his wonderous scent of fire and night as he fully invades my senses and lures me closer like a magnet to steel; inexplicably unable to remove to myself from his presence.

He's so close, I can feel him breathing and I sense the rhythm of my heartbeat increase at his proximity, something which entirely throws me mentally off balance. He's much taller than me so my head only comes to just beneath his chin as I slowly peer up and look into his eyes. His dark and stormy eyes meet mine unexpectedly as I face him and we still for only a moment

– locked in this trance together.

I entertain a thousand possibilities in my disordered brain as we continue to stare at each other in silence for which feels like an eternity in my anxious mind.

I stare at him and he stares back at me with an intense, yet indecipherable look. He has a look in his eyes I cannot translate when he halts my reckless train of thoughts and repeats: "Where are you going?"

"I'm going home." I sigh, slightly calmer as my defence mechanisms undertake a slow withdrawal into the back seat of my mind.

"Why aren't you going home with your friends?" he enquires.

"I can take care of myself," I state bluntly as I turn and continue walking, my magenta boots stomping loudly on the gravel path as I shift my bag higher on my shoulder in a futile attempt to adjust the weight of my world.

"Can I walk you home?" he asks quietly as I pick up my pace.

I hear his footsteps quicken behind me. "You can't walk home alone," he continues as he gently grabs my arm to stop me on my crusade. I shudder and shake him off. "Don't touch me, please," I plead quietly as I shake my arm out of his grip and move away from him. He lets go instantly and stares at me with a shocked expression, one I cannot entirely decipher once again. His facial expression is perplexing although, internally I wrestle with the very real thought that: "I think I hurt him in some way perhaps with my abrupt response." I ponder this quietly to myself as I turn and continue to walk away from him.

He doesn't follow this time.

"I don't even know his name." I sigh, kicking the dirt helplessly with my own combat boots. I hug myself tightly around my black corset for warmth and wander home silently within the inky blackness.

    Every. Single. Thought.
    All. The. Way. Home
    Is. About. Him.

Isabelle

The next morning, I wake up exhausted; mentally and physically completely drained.

I wash my face, brush my teeth and make my way to the kitchen – the house is eerily quiet. I'm normally not scared but today I feel so very alone. My parent's holiday house is not so small, it has seven bedrooms and five bathrooms with all the modern luxuries; gym, theatre, spa, sauna and library. Being here alone, you can hear the house creak as it expands and contracts throughout the day with the intense heatwaves followed by dramatic rainstorms.

I turn on the outside speakers to play some music, attempting to alleviate the thoughts of being utterly alone and chase away the demons that plague me today. Sometimes I feel as though the devil himself is sitting right on my shoulder, whispering taunting remarks directly into my head to dissuade me from my future goals and plans. I brush them away today as I walk out the patio doors and lounge into the outdoor couches with my camera, intending to search through my most recent photos.

I have an interview tomorrow with a local magazine, the job sounds relatively easy however I have zero professional experience. I am hoping instead – they notice the detail and beauty within the photos I have taken for my submission.

The job includes providing background photos for the magazine which is a lifestyle and home edition published once a month, and it appears to be quite popular locally.

The role requires specific images, such as local gardens and sceneries to be captured, with a special focus on local businesses and attractions in each monthly issue. I complete my portfolio, adding the finishing touches which takes up most of the day, carefully editing the final images and then drifting off into an afternoon nap to forget.

The relentless drumming through my head today is like a full-blown parade, a symphony of anxious thoughts in a well-orchestrated procession throughout my mind.

Sleep gifts me an escape, blissfully allowing me to hide away from own thoughts as I drift away.

Maverick

"Why the long face Son?" Walter interrupts my thoughts as he moves through the warehouse and out to the roof top decking.

"It's nothing," I reply, lying to him as I lay on the roof deck with my guitar on my lap.

"Well... You know something Mav? If you bottle everything up inside – someday you will explode." He laughs heartily as he plonks himself down onto the lounge next to me.

"Walter, can I ask you something?" I ask sheepishly, not knowing if I should ask after the last attempt which only caused him an incredible amount of pain and sadness.

"Anything Mav, you know that?" He replies softly with a smile. "No matter how hard life gets, communication is an important tool at our disposal," he elaborates.

"Ahh," I sigh. "Thanks Walter, well... this may be incredibly difficult for you but I've been wondering about your son." I pause and try to find the right words to convey exactly what I need to understand whilst Walter sits up a little straighter, giving me his full attention. "If you had a choice, on the night your son tragically passed; would you rather he had been with you on that fateful night, or out with his friends experiencing life – as it were?" I ask as I put my guitar down, perching it softly against the outdoor lounge. I sit up to face Walter to give him my complete concentration, patiently awaiting his response, even though it is entirely not something I am sure I am ready to hear, nor he is ready to give.

Walter takes a deep breath and looks to his feet and then slowly back at me as he turns. "Maverick, to be honest, I would give anything to have one more moment with my son, the only regret I have is that I never got to say goodbye to him. Life throws us some deeply painful events that test our strength, patience and enduring love, but I know deep in my heart I am content that he spent his short life being happy; seeing his friends, fixing bikes and loving every minute of every day. He was at a happy place in his life when he died." He smiles at me sadly. "So, to answer your question Mav, I would rather he was with his friends, and doing what he loves most before his life was tragically taken away from us."

"Does that make sense to you Maverick?" Walter asks as he slowly wipes a tear from his face.

"Yeah Walter, it kind of does," I reply quietly.

"Look Mav, I don't know what's happened in your life, or what is happening, but you don't need to do it alone. I am here for you," Walter explains as he squeezes my shoulder and moves back towards the kitchen, silently filling the watering can to water the indoor plants in the warehouse, returning to his usual routine without question.

I'm so completely touched by Walter's caring, forgiving and sincere nature. His presence in my life makes me feel much less like the asshole I believe I am. He brings a smile to everyone he encounters and I believe, with a tiny sliver of hope, perhaps I can learn from him and grow into a better human.

"Perhaps with his wisdom and kindness, slowly illuminating my path ahead – I can navigate through the unbounded darkness that is me." I think about this hopefully to myself as I silently consider his own circumstances. "Everything he held dear – has been so tragically taken from him; his son, his wife, even his beloved dog, yet Walter always sees the good in the universe, and extraordinarily – people." I cannot fathom his level of faith as he takes every opportunity despite adversity, and consciously chooses to shine brighter every day as though he expects it to be better than the next, with no guarantee that it will actually happen.

"Hey... Walter!" I yell as he finishes watering and reaches the front door of the warehouse. "The world needs more people like you." I smile at him as I lean over the couch and peer down the stairs. Walter looks up and nods, tipping his hat forward and smiling as he steps through the door.

The week moves quickly as I busy myself with learning new songs and helping Walter at his music store. I find myself surprisingly learning; patience to deal with others, embracing new instruments that entirely capture me with their unique, yet impressive sounds, and understanding a little better that we all battle our own fierce internal wars. As we rage against ourselves everyday – we have no right to judge others and what battle they are fighting against. All we can do is be there to support them, if and when they want our help.

As the week fades away, I still have an intense niggling pain in my head. Pain sears through my brain and into my eyes frequently this week; it feels as though a hurricane is circulating wildly within my mind, barrelling closer and closer to my eyes with a sustained resolve, raining down unrelenting pain on me as I wince and lay back down into the outdoor lounge for the third time this week. At these times I think very carefully about my next decisions before I close my eyes to oblivion, attempting to escape the inevitable hurricane swirling within me.

Isabelle

"Hi Mum, guess what?" I exclaim excitedly down the phone.
"What honey?" she replies interested.
"I. Got. The. Job," I announce proudly down the phone.
"Oh Isabelle, that's wonderful news, let me get your father to tell him," she gushes.

"Hey Love," Dad's voice beams down the phone. "I heard you got the photography job with the magazine?" he asks proudly.

"Yeah, Dad I did. I am so proud that I did it all by myself, I worked so hard and I am so happy," I reply. I feel like jumping up and down on the spot with excitement and relief.

"I'm happy for you too sweetheart," he replies softly. His voice is translucent though, it is like he is lost within his own thoughts as a silence breezes through the phone.

"What's wrong Dad? You don't sound very happy?" I ask. Dad pauses, I can picture him running his hand through his hair whilst he carefully considers his response. "We are very much alike in everything we do; our responses and reactions always seem like a mirror image." I consider this as I await his response. "I'm happy love, it just means you'll be staying away for a bit longer," he explains sadly.

His words genuinely tug at my heart strings. I have been so wrapped up in myself that I'd forgotten to consider how my decisions would impact anyone else. "Oh Dad, I will come home soon for a visit, please don't worry." I stress, my mind racing.

"I'm not that far away at all. I love you Dad," I state.

My excitement of getting a job that truly inspires me and ignites my passion has now evolved into a worried tension. As much I am attempting to shut everyone out from my pain, I am now hurting other people with my haphazard decisions. "That was never my intention." I sigh to myself as I end the call.

I take a moment to think about the impacts of my decisions as I move into the kitchen, intending to make dinner. I reach into the fridge to explore my options, although now realising – there is nothing in the fridge, at all.

"Perfect." I state. "Completely empty like the rest of me." I contemplate this as I consider another rash decision to venture out. It is Friday night, and only early I think as I weigh my options quickly. Best case scenario; I enjoy the night and worst case scenario… well, channelling Flynn he would argue: *"There are no bad options darling – only lessons to be learned on our journey. Lessons that will make us whole again with time."*

I head into my room searching for something to wear that does not involve jumpers or tracksuit pants (staples I never thought would be in my vocabulary ever as I wrestle with my internal recluse). "I need to hear him again," I breathe. I sit on the bed and weigh my options carefully again in my distressed mind; I stay here and overthink all of my fearful thoughts, or I take control and do something that makes me happy – if only for a fleeting moment in time. His voice took me away, very faraway to another place, a place of awe, yet feelings of tranquillity and peace enveloped me as he performed. I would give anything just to hear him sing again, regardless if it is in evanescence.

"Decision made." I smile to myself.

Isabelle

I push open the heavy barn door of the bar as smoke reaches my eyes and I struggle to adjust to the brightness of the room. I scan the room as quickly as I can for a seat and locate one near the front of the stage in a booth near the window. I peel off my warm jacket and belongings, placing them haphazardly across the table and wander over to the bar to order.

"Alone tonight gorgeous?" Luna asks as I reach the bar.

"Yeah, the fridge is empty and home is too quiet tonight," I reply as I place my arms up onto the bar. Luna flicks her long dark wavy hair and smiles.

"No problems, I will fix you something to eat, take a seat lovely." She smiles genuinely.

"Thanks Luna," I reply and turn to walk away back to the booth.

"Hey Isabelle?" Luna calls from behind me, "Are you okay?" she questions.

I turn and smile. "I'm fine Luna, I promise," I reply with a real honest answer this time. She shrugs her shoulders and turns to walk back out into the kitchen.

I like Luna, she's beautiful and down to earth. She is studying to be a doctor but works here part time to earn some extra cash to support her six-year old son, and her medical studies. She has seen people at their very worst but never intrudes on my own personal journey. I can only assume she sees all kinds of trouble working in a bar, although I know that she is genuinely a good human with the kindest of hearts. She carries herself with the strength of a lion – always protecting her cub, although maintains the illusion of a poker face – whereby no one will ever truly understand her emotions as they are locked deeply away, hidden behind her well-built facade, a disguise I understand and know all too well.

The sounds of his distinctive melody reach my ears within the hour and I close my eyes to feel the depth of the music. I realise I feel completely at peace within this moment, a brief respite within my complicated and puzzling mind that is both surprising, and yet a welcome relief.

I listen intently as he strums the guitar for a few minutes, getting the chords right before he starts his first set. He doesn't look up as I sit staring, (borderline inappropriately) gazing directly at him as he begins his first song: MGMT: Kids. It is a slower, acoustic version as I listen in rapture through the verses and choruses. He completely captivates my attention as he sings the lyrics and plays the song in the most haunting, yet beautiful way.

He glances up, noticing me during the song as his midnight eyes slowly reach mine. "I should look away," I breathe, but I cannot as he continues to stare back at me from the stage.

He is perched on a bar stool, his guitar resting perfectly on his knee before the microphone stand. I am utterly captivated by him as I momentarily wash away my fears to be present in this moment. It's like an understanding of some kind passes between us, I should nod or move or even blink, but the moment is too perfect – I stare at him and he gazes back for what feels infinite.

Luna interrupts our unspoken interaction and my solace as she delivers a crisp salad and crunchy fries to my booth.

"Looks like he's finally woken up," she states as she places the plate on the table and looks over to the singer.

"What do you mean?" I ask Luna curiously.

"Maverick." She indicates to the singer. "He plays twice, sometimes three times a week, but barely speaks to anyone, just plays his heart out and leaves. He's constantly shooing the female admirers away, but he seems to have seen something he likes." She smiles and looks back towards me with a wink, then turns and waltzes back to the bar.

"Maverick, such a beautiful name for a beautiful voice," I think to myself as I stir the chips around on my plate, contemplating everything Luna has just said.

"Just enjoy life's moments Belle, don't overthink." Flynn chimes into my memories, jolting me from my internal deconstruction of Luna's words whilst I continue to toss the fries helplessly around my plate. I tune back into my surroundings and listen to him play in rapture, completely fascinated by each and every single word that leaves his lips.

The night hours disappear quickly, before I know it – it's already close to midnight and the place is bursting at the seams. I hardly noticed the rowdy crowd growing throughout the night as I was listening so intently to every set Maverick played. After he finishes, and has long since left the stage, I sit silently tuning out the world and think for a while to myself. I attempt to process my new confusing thoughts: "Why am I here? Not physically here in this bar, more here – at this exact time and space in life. Was every event leading me here? Is this where I am supposed to be? Where do I want to be?" Such difficult questions I ask myself as the crowd surges with the DJ now taking the stage. I slowly grab my jacket, wrap my satchel over my shoulder and around my waist as I scoot out of the booth towards the front door.

I pull on my jacket and wrap my fluffy collar and hood up to surround me as I move to press forward through the crowd, slowly moving towards the exit and out into the almost winter night.

I freeze in my tracks, my steps faltering as I look up and notice Maverick is standing there, holding the door open for me as he gestures with his right hand the way out. Maverick holds the door frame with his left hand high above me, with a single eyebrow raise and a dangerous smirk he looks directly at me. I hesitate, standing motionless as I stare back at him.

"He's not asking you to walk barefoot through the burning lava of Mount Vesuvius Isabelle, he's gesturing you to walk through a door." I internally laugh nervously to myself as my emotions run wild and my brain is caught in a dramatic thunderstorm. He waits patiently as I finally end my internal argument and walk through the door, brushing gently past him and whispering a barely audible, "Thank you."

"You're welcome," he whispers as he bends down and speaks dangerously close to my ear in his rich deep voice.

I feel my heart speed up with his proximity, his dark and stormy scent matches his mysteriousness as it once again invades my senses. He completely breaks my mind – with only two simple words. "Get a grip Isabelle," I laugh at myself. I can only imagine Flynn, peeling with laughter at my inept ability to function like a normal adult at the simplest of interactions.

"Can I walk you home?" he interrupts my barrel of inappropriate thoughts, more of a statement than a question.

"That's not really a good idea," I stammer as I turn and stop to look him in the eye, shrugging my winter jacket higher in a futile attempt to hide me, and my fragile emotions.

"Well neither was you walking home alone the other night." He raises his eyebrow in question as I inspect the small bar pierced through his eyebrow with two small balls on either end. Such a tiny statement that coexists with his lip ring which is incredibly attractive, adding to his mysterious persona. I consider his question and latter statement carefully. "Umm... okay well sure, I guess that's okay," I stumble out. "But why do you want to walk me home?" I elaborate. "I am fairly certain you have a million other things you could be doing?" I question this, unsure of myself and this entire situation. "Is this safe decision?" I hesitate to myself.

"Trust your instincts angel." Flynn's voice echoes in my ear as a thousand drastic thoughts continue to run though my head. I attempt to channel Flynn again to chase away my negative thoughts (and perhaps prevent me from fleeing in this moment). Flynn was always best at battling my demons and I think running away from Maverick, in the car park, at the local bar, would be an epic, all new level of ridiculousness – even for me.

"You're so incredibly strong Isabelle, take chance on life and give it real go. You've got this princess – I believe in you." Flynn states softly as I recall his words and the memories of us. We were laying on the beach with my head resting gently on his chest as the waves crashed against the shore. I remember the moment perfectly as the magnificent sun was setting ever so slowly on that given day. It was a magical display of deep oranges and vivid reds, the intertwined colours ever so slowly dipping deep below the rich blue waves – as he unobtrusively instilled his sound advice. To this day, I still truly appreciate his guidance, attempting to apply his wisdom with every decision I make.

"I thought I might enjoy your company." Maverick interrupts my internal montage as he smiles down at me.

"Are you going to murder me and throw me in the lake?" I add. Maverick looks at me with an amused expression until he bursts out laughing.

"You ask me now? After you've already agreed to me walking you home?" He is still laughing as he turns and starts walking down the gravel pathway.

"I didn't fully agree!" I protest as I march after him in my magenta boots.

The walk is silent for a few minutes other than our footsteps crunching across the gravel. It's not an awkward silence, just a silence until he finally asks, "What is your name?" I peek up at him as he slides his hand through his raven hair and peers slowly to his right to look at me.

"Isabelle," I reply quietly, returning my gaze to the sandy path in front of me – anywhere but looking at him.

"I'm Maverick, Maverick Black. And Isabelle, it is a pleasure to meet you." He smiles as I peek back up at him whilst he speaks.

"Do you mind if we stop at my place and drop my guitar off?" he asks as he glances sideways at me again.

"Ahh. Hell. No!" My instincts scream internally at me. I hesitate, feeling instantly uncertain.

I believe he senses my shift in demeanour as my brain instantly switches from: "calm walk home to serial killer escape mode," terrified as my steps falter. Mavericks stops walking and confidently takes a step to stand a little closer as he looks directly at me. Maverick shifts his guitar case and gently leans on it, the only object separating us as he slowly rubs his hand through his hair. "I'm not going to hurt you Isabelle," he states with sincerity in his tone. "If you don't want to, that's completely fine. I just thought it may be easier," he continues.

"Oh sure, it's no problem at all. I don't mind," I whisper quietly even though my brain is screaming 'no' – in a thousand different ways.

We make the rest of the journey in silence to his place until we arrive at a large double story warehouse. It has impressive black framed windows, situated up so incredibly high in which I would imagine has the most magnificent views across the lake. I stand out the front staring up at the building in awe as Maverick makes his way up the side stair case, heading towards what I assume is the front door.

He stops mid-stride, his black combat boots slamming down on the metal steps with a resounding thud. "Are you coming Isabelle?" He questions, raising his eyebrow ring slightly which makes my insides flutter.

"I can just wait here," I yell up the steps as I hug myself for warmth. Now we have stopped moving, I feel the wind whip around my face and send a chill deep into my bones. He marches back down the steps purposefully and faces me, close enough for me to inhale his scent. "Isabelle, I'm not going to hurt you, and it's probably safer inside than standing here in the middle of the street, in the dark, at half past midnight."

"Said every serial killer ever known." I think to myself. "I will be fine. I can take care of myself, you know?" I blurt back.

"I know. I'm not doubting your capabilities Isabelle, however if I'm walking you home, I want to do my best to make sure you get there safely." He smirks as he holds out his hand and stands patiently waiting for me to decide.

I look up as he smiles his brilliant teeth at me. I feel like my little black heart has awoken and taken a thousand beats instantaneously. I have no words as this moment feels intimate –

yet I hardly know him. It is his music which makes me feel as though our souls do already know each other. It is although they were destined to meet, crash right onto one another's paths and connect like stars, hooked on a particular destination that slams right into each other; exploding in the night like a brilliant display of magnetism and fate.

I'm holding my breath as I decide to take his hand, feeling his warmth as his hand slides gently into mine and he slowly motions me towards the staircase. I tentatively follow up him the metal staircase, his hand is secure within mine and he doesn't let go as he opens the door, gesturing to let me walk in first. "Beautiful and has manners," I smile to myself.

I stand slightly inside the doorway and look around, it is not at all what I expected. It's not dark like his personality, it's full of light, open space and vivid colours. Brilliant downlights illuminate the area which highlight the beautiful, deep burgundy feature walls and a large open fire place. Impressive timber glass French doors span the whole back wall leading to an alfresco area. An intricate timber staircase leads up to another level and a state-of-the-art kitchen stands proudly on the lower level.

"I won't be a minute," he calls as he leans his guitar case next to the hall stand and walks down the hallway to what I'm assuming could be his bedroom or bathroom perhaps.

I place myself on a bar stool at his kitchen island bench, looking around, unsure of what I should be doing aside from admiring his immaculate kitchen and fancy toaster. He comes back out placing a hoodie over his head. "Do you want another jacket, Isabelle?" He asks as he stops mid-stride, attempting to pull his hoodie down. It's tugging his t-shirt up giving me an impressive view of his perfect abs whilst he struggles to untangle the two.

"Isabelle?" he asks again with a wide smirk on his face. He's caught me staring, admiring his perfect body and heat rushes to my face at my realisation. "Oh no, I'm fine thanks," I stutter, trying to drag myself away from my wildly inappropriate thoughts about his body.

"Can I see outside?" I ask pointing to the French doors.

"Sure," he replies making his way over as he picks up his guitar and slides open the expansive glass doors.

There is a couch and two sun lounges with a small table in the middle. Maverick walks over and lights the candle within the glass holder on the table. It illuminates the space perfectly as I walk closer to the balustrade and peer over the balcony, I can see the tree tops swaying gently in the night sky, during the daylight I would imagine that the lake would shimmer proudly just beyond those trees.

Maverick lounges into the couch. The couch is old and sunken I observe as I make my way over and sit down gently beside him, breathing in the crisp night air. I sink deep down into the couch which allows me to lean back and stare straight up into the sky. "It's beautiful," I state quietly as the night sky is clear and filled with billions of stars. The sight makes me smile, it's untouched and beyond beautiful.

Maverick slides up, adjusting as he places his guitar in his hands, resting it gently on his lap. "You play and sing like an angel," I say to him as I continue gazing up at the mystical night sky.

"Yeah, you think so?" he replies, unsure of himself.

"Yes," I state, feeling a little more confident as I no longer feel the need to flee. "I wish I had half as much talent as you." I sigh, "but I don't like to be noticed, so count me out of any entertaining job." I laugh softly.

Maverick is not laughing as he strums his guitar. "You should be noticed Isabelle," he states and starts to play Dermott Kennedy 'Better Days' with the most beautiful melody. Tears well in my eyes as he sings softly with emotion and passion. Not a single part of him is not involved in his music – his soul laid bare as he continues and a tear slowly rolls down my face.

My emotions bubble to the surface, unable to stop my tears as the words of the song resonate deeply within me. Maverick stops playing, resting his guitar on the other side of him and gently pulls me a little closer towards him. I let him, without fear or hesitation in that moment as I lean my head on his chest and wipe away my tears.

I feel his hand stroking my hair softly, my eyes are heavy with the memories and burden of me. I close them slowly as he continues to finish the song, singing softly without his guitar. Just him alone, releasing the quiet, yet powerful words.

I think he's the perfect version of me.

Maverick

My legs feel heavy as I shift slightly to get comfortable.
"Fuck," I curse quietly. She's lying on my lap sleeping. She fidgets around and speaks slowly and painfully. "Don't. Wait please, Elijah," she whispers as she continues to move around.
She is warm, her entire body feels hot as I place my palm gently on her cheek. "She's having a bad dream." I exhale. "Isabelle," I urge quietly in her ear. "Isabelle, wake up. You're having a bad dream," I whisper and shake her gently to rouse her from the dream.
I don't even know her and usually I'm a complete asshole regardless, however there is something unique and different about her. I felt a magnetic pull towards her ever since I spotted her during my one of my sets, intrigued by her as I watched her march up to the bar in those absurd magenta boots. They made me smile as she wore them with such pride. She has a fascinating aurora surrounding her, captivating my attention – although tonight has certainly shown me, no matter how bright her light is – she also has her own demons to battle.
Isabelle opens her eyes and attempts to focus. She moves upright quickly and backs into the corner of the couch with her knees pulled up to her chest. She sits motionless staring at me and appears afraid. Her blue eyes open wide, like a deer in the headlights of an oncoming car, stunned and unable to move.
I move and kneel down in front of the couch, attempting to alleviate her fear. "Isabelle, you had a bad dream, are you okay?"

She nods her head slowly. "Come," I say quietly as I stand and extend my hand out to hers, although she doesn't move. "Isabelle, I promise you, I'm not going to hurt you. It's cold out here, let's go inside," I state as she reluctantly takes my hand and shifts her legs slowly onto the floor.

I grab both her hands in mine and lead her into the house, down the hallway and into my room. She sits on the edge of the bed, again with her knees pulled up tightly to her chest and her arms wrapped securely around them. I kneel down and look her in the eyes, she's somewhere else entirely right now, lost in her own thoughts. "Fuck, this is a very bad idea," I think to myself but my options are limited. It's very late, I don't have a car and I certainly wouldn't trust some ride sharing service with her while she's vulnerable.

We don't speak as I move the covers and gently ease her under, pulling the blanket up to her shoulders. I wander over to the bathroom to freshen up and then climb in the other side of the bed. I'm fully clothed, the obvious decision as I don't want to freak her out, or for her to get the wrong impression so I keep my jeans on and all, no matter how uncomfortable. "Jesus, who am I?" I laugh quietly to myself, knowing I've never slept next to a woman fully clothed in my life.

I lay my head on the pillow and close my eyes as I feel her shift and roll over. She's now laying incredibly close. I feel her body warmth and inhale her scent as I feel her arm reach across my abdomen. I move my arm up and she shifts her head to lie within my arms and on my chest, I hug her close to me and kiss the top of her head gently not to rouse her. I don't know what has happened to her, but she's hurting and she seems a little bit lost.

I understand what it is to be lost, and I understand pain, but I am entirely the wrong person she needs.

Maverick

I wake up feeling incredibly tired. I think I tried to stay awake as long as possible last night, listening to the gentle rhythm of her heartbeat on my chest as she slept. I adjust my jeans, they are entirely the most fucking uncomfortable thing I've ever slept in.

I open my eyes and turn my head and I'm left with a confused and empty feeling. She's gone. "She must have left when I fell asleep this morning," I determine. I didn't for a second assume she would be in my kitchen making coffee, wearing only one of my shirts. "Fuck I'm so wound up. She plagues my thoughts and now my body." I sigh.

Questions race through my mind for the rest of the morning. Every. Single. Thought.
Is. About. Her....

Isabelle

I race home to grab my camera and portfolio. "I'm going to be late," I stress as I rush to brush my mangled hair, tying it into a loose braid, touching up my makeup and attempting to look respectable for my first assignment for the magazine.

The editor wants me to start today, Saturday. "Of all days to start a new job!" I curse.

The editor thinks that I need to start on Saturday, indicating I will need some sort of a crowd for the shots he requested for my first work assignment, and the park is guaranteed to always be filled on Saturdays. So, I agreed, even though I already know what type of photos I want to capture for the story he's given me.

The rest of the morning I spend at the park, taking as many images as possible. I capture the beauty of the surrounds and the effervescent crowd as they enjoy the weekend local vendors and the magnificent lake. I eventually lie down on the cool grass in the sun and close my eyes. I feel my stomach tingle as I remember last night.

"He is so incredible." I smile remembering Maverick holding me close, how gentle and warm he was, coupled with his intoxicating scent – just as dark and mysterious as he is.

"That... was a stupid, very stupid thing to do Isabelle." My rational brain scolds myself, regardless of the butterflies in my stomach. "No matter how wonderful, you don't even know him and you allowed yourself to be vulnerable. It will never happen again." I assure myself.

I wander home very slowly, there really is no hurry as I enjoy walking and being outside in the fresh air, it always helps clear my mind. I pluck my headphones out of my satchel and pull out my playlist, scrolling through the options as I flick through my favourites and turn the volume up to maximum. I sing along out loud all the way home. I don't even care who sees me this time as I smile happily to myself.

I'm now singing along to Kings Of Leon as if I'm the lead singer, pouring my heart out as I waltz down the long gravel driveway to my house. I sing louder than usual as it's one of my favourites. I reach into my satchel and feel around for my keys, my fingers grasp the key chain and I yank them from my bag as I look up to the front door.

I suddenly drop the keys in the gravel and slowly peel my headphones off, laying them gently around my neck as I realise Maverick is sitting on my front steps – laughing blissfully at me.

"That was wonderful Isabelle, you should sing with me at the bar." He claps as he smiles and stands up, leaning on a front pillar, arms crossed with one leg in front of the other. He looks irresistible in his tight ripped jeans, black shirt, menacing black combat boots, and his messy dark hair washing over his eye as he plays with his lip ring, twirling it through his fingers.

"What are you doing here?" I ask. "And how do you know where I live?" I also ask before he can answer. I stand there, hands on hips, awaiting an answer. He looks down and shoves his hands in his pockets.

"Well… you took off this morning, and I was worried about you. Perhaps I overstepped an invisible line?" he questions honestly. "I offered to walk you home safely and… well you know the rest. So, I just wanted to make sure you were okay." He stands silently, waiting to see my reaction.

"Well, I believe we have had this conversation before Mr Black, and I can assure you, I can take of myself and again – how do you know where I live?" I question.

"I asked Luna at the bar." He smirks.

"Great," I reply. "So much for neighbourhood watch," I state as I move past him to open the front doors.

"Would you like to come in?" I ask quietly as I unceremoniously place my bag on the hall stand and move towards the kitchen. Maverick follows me in slowly, closing the door gently whilst taking in the surroundings.

"You're really something else you know that?" he questions, although his intent seems unclear in my mind.

"What does that mean?" I ask defensively, a little confused by his statement.

"You come for dinner at the local bar and hang out with less than desirable people, but you live here – in a *mansion*. I'm waiting to see the maids appear and start dusting the vases." He winks at me as he leans against the kitchen island, his response making me genuinely laugh with relief.

"This belongs to my parents, not me. I don't own a single thing in here apart from a few clothes and necessities," I reply.

"Where are you parents?" he asks as he turns to look at the pictures hung on the walls. The pictures are of me and my siblings predominantly, some of Mum and Dad and relatives we rarely see.

"They are at home. This is their holiday house," I state.

"So… you are only here for a short time then?" he asks curiously.

"I don't know." I answer honestly. "I'm not ready to go home yet, and I just got a job at a local magazine, so I'm here until I change my mind. What about you?" I ask inquisitively.

"What about me?" he replies with a smug smile.

"Well... I know you live in a warehouse, and sing at the local. That's all I know about you?" I question, stating the obvious – which sounds a million times worse as I say it aloud.

He laughs and moves over to the sliding doors to see the view outside the back window. "Yep, that's all you know about me, and you let me attempt to walk you home, you come into a stranger's house *and*... sleep in his bed." He smiles as he turns to look at me. "Not that I'm complaining," he adds, hands up in the air in surrender. "But you should be more careful Isabelle."

"I know." I sigh, feeling the depth of his words. "But... You did sleep with your jeans on." I laugh uncontrollably as he smiles broadly, catching on as he turns towards me whilst I spin and run down the hallway laughing.

"That's not fair Isabelle, I didn't want to scare you." He laughs as he chases after me. I reach the back-laundry door and unsnap the lock as I race down the backyard embankment, racing towards the lake.

He's too quick. I feel his powerful arms wrap around me as he grabs me and quickly swoops me into his arms, my body is lifted swiftly off the ground with my knees cradled safely in his arms, and my own arms braced tightly around his neck. "You think that's funny, do you Isabelle?" He asks as he holds me close and whispers in my ear, "well... let's see how funny this is," he states as he jogs towards the lake. I make a futile protest, unable to stop laughing long enough to argue my case from his arms.

"Don't even think about Maverick!" My legs are swinging wildly as he genuinely smiles at me, "Can you swim Isabelle?" he asks. I laugh harder, happy memories fill my mind as I recall the countless summers my sister and I have spent here – jumping from the end of this very jetty into the fresh water. "Yes of course

I can." I reply as throws me unceremoniously into the water from the end of the jetty. I come up laughing and coughing water, my hair is awkwardly stuck to my face as Maverick lazes on the grass with a dangerously attractive smile.

I move slowly out of the water, grabbing my shirt and wringing it out. "I can't remember the last time I was this genuinely happy." I smile as I walk closer until I'm standing directly beside him. Maverick winks at me as he lays on his back in the lush grass, hands behind his head, with a body that would cause a riot.

I decide this game is not quite over just yet with a devilish idea as I move closer and plant my body firmly on his, ensuring all the water now seeps into his clothes as he squirms and starts laughing harder. "Now, we are even," I state with a satisfied smile as I move to inspect how well I had achieved the sharing of my water-soaked clothes with his.

He grabs my hands and pulls me back down towards him gently. I'm now straddling him as he moves his body, sitting upright to face me. We sit connected in silence, he's stopped laughing as he reaches up to move my wet hair out of my eyes and away from my face. I can feel him breathing. I inhale his scent of fire and night – so dangerous and mysterious, it suits him perfectly as I feel my heart beat faster within my chest. This impromptu moment has now turned into something more, much more intimate than I imagined when letting him into my kitchen earlier.

He places his hand on my cheek and I take a deep breath as he moves closer, his lips touch mine and he slowly kisses me. "Tell me to 'stop' Isabelle and I will," he breathes. I don't answer. It's like being hit with tiny electric currents, the effect ripples throughout my body as my body shivers with need. I can feel his lip ring and it is so sensual, I absolutely don't want him to stop. My mind is anxious, but I know in this very moment – I don't want to be anywhere else but here.

Maverick kisses me so passionately, he's like a wild storm that I don't want to run away from. I want more. "Isabelle," he growls in response to his earlier unanswered question. "Maverick, don't stop," I whisper between us. I think he feels my tension, although I try to keep my anxiety at bay – I want to be here in this moment with him.

He breaks away slowly, as he kisses gently down my cheek making his way towards my neck with his hands pulling me closer. I feel completely on fire right now, I entirely want to peel his clothes off here on the back lawn regardless of how inappropriate. I feel him harden beneath me and I know he feels the same as he slowly trails kisses back up my neck. I move my hands to his face, letting him take control as his hands shift behind me pulling me even closer to him.

Maverick slowly stops kissing me and pulls us apart slightly so he can see me. "Are you okay?" he whispers.

"Yes Maverick, I'm perfect," I reply as I stare into his stormy eyes and move in to kiss his lips again.

Maverick

I visit Isabelle countless times over the next few months. She's incredibly smart and beautiful and I'm completely drawn to her – I feel an inexplicable pull towards her like two magnets destined to be connected. "I know I need to back away before I hurt her. Fuck, I just don't know how. I should never have pursued her – this can only end with broken hearts and shattered dreams." I sigh sadly to myself as I walk up Isabelle's driveway.

"Did you bring your guitar?" she asks as she opens the front doors with a huge smile on her face. She takes my breath away each and every time I see her. She has long blonde wavy hair which hangs down past her shoulders, coupled with the most brilliant blue eyes that pierce straight through me and the most incredible body I have ever laid eyes upon. I find it exceedingly difficult to concentrate on anything other than her and reign in my primal desires when she is close. Although, I would never make an unwanted advance, ever.

It is apparent Isabelle has not one shred of self-confidence and I don't completely know why. My assumptions lead me to believe that someone, or something – hurt her so badly that she has built up a solid barrier, fiercely protecting herself. I consider this carefully as I'm finding it very difficult to break though Isabelle's pain – her impenetrable fortress walls – built strategically around her heart. She appears to bottle her pain inside, only letting our conversations flow onto other topics – nothing personal ever.

"What's wrong Mav?" she asks concerned as I realise I haven't even responded to her initial question.

"Sorry Isabelle, yeah I brought my guitar. Are you sure you want to do this?" I ask her curiously.

"Yep, Yep, Yep," she replies jumping up and down and clapping excitedly.

I enjoy nothing more than making her smile. "Come on," she says as she pulls my hand through the house excitedly, leading me outside to the back patio. "I'm ready," she laughs.

"Okay, hold on their kitten, you need to learn the basics first," I reply with a playful smile and a wink.

Isabelle has been asking me to teach her how to play the guitar, she said she needs to learn everything before she's old as she's wasted so many years already. She wouldn't elaborate on the "how" she wasted so many years, too personal once again, but I'll entertain the idea to make her happy. "Isabelle, I've been thinking about your guitar lessons and I want to play a little payback on the lessons." I smile. I thought of this idea last week when she refused to tell me who Elijah is. "I'm not giving you any sexual favours Maverick Black; So – Forget – It." She responds, emphasising the last part with a smug smile of victory as she crosses her arms defiantly over her chest.

Isabelle's extreme reaction makes me genuinely smile, although unwarranted in this situation, I am proud of her regardless, defending her own dignity and standing up for herself. I laugh internally at Isabelle's determined stance, 'our relationship', if you can even call it that, is a slow moving, sometimes confusing, yet explosive connection – although, Isabelle has her own demons that haunt her relentlessly. And I certainly don't want to pressure her into anything she is not ready for.

I want nothing more than to run my hands all over her body and pleasure her, until my name is the only one that will ever cross her lips. Surprisingly, I find myself wanting the experience of waking up with her in my arms – every – single – morning, but I know she has her limits right now, she's scared and healing.

"Your mind is always in the gutter Isabelle, I love it," I reply, shaking away my deeper thoughts and moving closer to her. "As much as I would love to provide you sexual pleasure, no, the payment will be something much more important. Every note you master in the guitar lessons, I get to ask you one personal question, which you will answer truthfully," I state.

Silence as her jaw actually drops. "Maverick, why do you want to know my private thoughts? You don't trust me?" she asks painfully.

"Isabelle, I want to know all of you, the good, the bad, the ugly. Not just the surface," I state. I try to gauge her reaction in her eyes as I continue. "It's not about trust, I undoubtedly trust you, but I want you to let me in Isabelle." That statement is entirely contradictory considering my own circumstances and what I'm keeping from her, but I never claimed to be a saint.

"Okay fine," she huffs, obviously not happy with the decision.

We play for hours and she seems to be struggling, she has not mastered a single thing. I sit behind her with my legs wrapped around hers as I reach around her to teach her the chords. The guitar rests softly on her legs as my hands move slowly and patiently with hers while she learns.

I start laughing and she stops practising, turning back towards me to see what is so funny with a curious look on her face. "Isabelle, are you sabotaging the lesson so I don't get to ask you a personal question?" I ask her honestly.

Isabelle bursts out laughing in hysterics, she can't stop laughing which brings a broad smile to my face. Isabelle laughs so hard that tears form in the corners of her eyes as she wipes them away and turns back again to face me. "No Mav, I'm not sabotaging anything, I really am this awful at guitar, some would say 'musically challenged'," she continues laughing.

"Well Miss Perfect, I do know something that you are exceptionally good at." I smile and move the guitar off her lap, placing it gently on the couch and scoot her around in my lap.

"What's that Mr Black?" she blushes as she asks with a smile, knowing exactly what I meant as I grab her face gently and pull her lips towards mine.

Kissing her is like a riot to my senses, her lips taste like strawberries and she smells absolutely incredible; a scent of orange blossoms with a hint of vanilla invades me every time I'm close to her. She kisses me back with just as much passion and fire in her veins as her hands reach under my shirt to my chest. Isabelle slowly tortures my senses as she runs her delicate hands up my chest and back down again. I can barely contain myself. I shift as I feel my need grow for her tenfold.

I take a deep breath and grab her hands gently from underneath my shirt and hold them within mine. "Isabelle." I groan.

"Please," she whispers into my lips. "I want this, I want you," she pleads. I rub her hands gently between mine and pull my face away from hers. I know I can't let this continue without telling her the real reason I am here in this town... and what I am hiding from her, from Walter, from everyone. It's a fucked-up situation but I cannot expect her to be vulnerable and honest – when I have been the complete opposite.

"Isabelle, there's something I need to tell you." I know this is going to hurt her, but I need to do it before it's too late to turn back. I've already waited too long. I have been a coward, hoping my secrets would indeed just fade away and disappear into the inky black nights.

She doesn't speak, as I rub her hands softly in silence. I need a moment to consider the right way to tell her this and carefully select the right words without destroying her completely.

I gently rub her wrists underneath her black and gold bands she wears every day. "They're like her trademark statement," I think to myself as my fingers grind across rough lines etched into her skin. I move my fingers backwards and forwards over the rough surface, curiosity emerging to understand what it is she is hiding under there. "It could only be a scar or birthmark?" I consider this as I run my fingers further down her wrists. Isabelle slowly pulls her hands away from me before I can go any further, sparking my curiosity like a flame.

I stop patiently and look up at her as she sits motionless on my lap. Unease covers her face as I gently grab her wrists again, seeking permission within her gaze. Isabelle slightly nods as she turns her hands over slowly and I pull the intricate wrist bands down towards her palms. She doesn't struggle against me as I attempt to absorb what I'm looking at, long jagged scars sliced into her skin, not a few but many of them. Some larger than others and they are also etched into her palms. Some scars look deep, others only fine lines. I consider this silently as she stares at me and then sadly back down at her hands.

As I attempt to comprehend what I'm looking at, feelings of anger rapidly rise to the surface. I'm very fucking angry, furious in fact – the very thought she would intentionally harm herself – feels like someone has plunged a knife deep into my chest.

I struggle to comprehend any of this as I gently move her away from my lap and stand up. "Why Isabelle?" I whisper angrily as I pace furiously in front of her.

She shies away from me and places her head down, her arms connect around her legs once again as she moves back into her own protective circle. She is completely silent, unable to look at me which only fuels my anger further. I need to leave before I do something chaotic and stupid, I pick up my guitar and turn to leave when I hear her whisper quietly, "Mav."

I stop briefly in my tracks, although realisation dawns on me, "I can't stop. I should not stop. I'm far too angry to talk right now," I seethe in my head as I march back through the house.

"Mav, it's not what you think, I promise."

Those are the last words I hear from her as I walk out of her home.

Isabelle

I cry myself to sleep outside on the lounge.

He's gone. Everything that is Maverick is gone. His scent, his laughter, his energy – our beautiful connection. He was so angry when he left, he was beyond furious in fact. I don't think I can ever face him again, not even to explain.

"There is always a way." Flynn's words attempt to give me hope. *"Don't ever give up beautiful. You should never give up. Now straighten that crown and pick yourself back up."*

Not even Flynn's words can pull me from my overwhelming sadness. I mope at home for what feels like a bleak stretch of infinity. In reality, it's two weeks, an incredibly slow moving two weeks that drains my soul.

I feel like an episode of the walking dead. Sleeping, crying, sleeping and more crying, moving as though I have no real purpose. I can't function at all. It's not like we were in a committed relationship, but his absence is felt as deep as the Veryovkina cave, and my emotions are completely lost within the darkest abyss.

Maverick brought something very unique and special into my life when I was lost and confused. His music, his laughter, his creative energy, and although somewhat dark and brutally honest at times; his thoughts were intellectually stimulating. Every experience we shared is irreplaceable and if I'm being completely honest – he made me feel entirely safe and protected when I was with him.

"I am utterly alone and devastatingly empty again," I think tragically. I cry every day at anything that even remotely reminds me of him – I cry at everything. It is impacting my ability to function and I feel myself sliding backwards off a steep cliff.

My painful memories resurface, a tormenting slide show that flickers past in my mind, threatening to devour me with each heart-rendering image. "There is no one around to care. I have effectively made sure of that as I pushed anyone and everyone – very far away from me when things got hard." I sigh helplessly to myself as I sit alone with my negative thoughts.

I created this disastrous mess and now I'm too afraid to fix it.

Isabelle

I'm woken to a loud and forceful banging on the front entry doors. I slowly pull myself up from the position I slumped into earlier and poke my head over the kitchen island bench. My hands clasp the stone bench top as I peer over it towards the front doors and listen carefully.

The banging is louder again. I wipe my face and walk slowly over to the door. "Open this door right now Isabelle! Or I'm going to break in, I swear to god!" Madison's voice echo's through the doors. "I know you're in there," she yells as I slowly make my way closer to unlock the deadbolt and pull the doors open.

"Oh my Isabelle, what happened? What did he do? I'm going to break his arms *and* his legs if he hurt you," Madison states determined as she pulls me into a fierce hug and then back out again, inspecting me for any sign of physical damage. I embrace her, wrapping my arms around her as I cry into her shoulder and she rubs my back peacefully.

"It wasn't him Madison, it was me," I sob.

Madison pulls me closer and wipes my tears away. "Isabelle, honey you need to stop shutting people out. You can't cry here alone, it's not good for you, you've come so far," she calmly whispers to me while I just nod. Madison inhales deeply before she continues, "I nearly lost it trying to find you. Isabelle, you don't answer your phone, you're not at work, you haven't been down the bar, I thought…" she trails off. Madison starts crying now too.

"I thought something terrible had happened to you…and I would never see you again," she whispers.

After a long embrace and few minutes in silence together, Madison places a kiss on my cheek as she pulls away and moves into the butler's pantry. Once she finally emerges she asks quietly: "So… are you going to tell me what happened?" Madison prompts as she starts sweeping up with the dustpan and brush, cleaning up the shards of broken glass on the kitchen floor. Madison works silently, patiently awaiting a response as she sweeps, she doesn't question the destruction and I don't offer an answer for it, knowing, I was the one who threw the glass at the kitchen wall last week in utter despair. I will admit – it was certainly not my finest moment.

"Oh Madison, I ruined everything," I reply, placing my head in my hands as I slide down the kitchen bench and sit helplessly on the floor whilst she cleans.

"I'm sure you didn't beautiful. I know he's hurting just as much as you are Isabelle, your both probably too stubborn to realise it." She smiles.

"How do you know that?" I ask curiously.

"Well… Cruize said something's been off with Maverick. He didn't play last week, and he was in a foul mood when Cruize went to talk to him. Cruize asked if Mav knew where you were as he'd seen you and him spending some time together in between his sets a couple of weeks earlier." She raises her eyebrow at me with the 'You *should* have told me' look. "Maverick blew him off without a response so when I told Cruize I couldn't reach you by phone, he was worried that he hadn't seen you around either – not even down the park. We panicked Isabelle and I flew here straight away." She explains. "Cruize has been over a couple of times to check on you but you never answered," she finishes sadly as she looks down and continues sweeping.

I pull the 'O' face at her. "I didn't think anyone would notice," I think to myself. "I'm so sorry Madison, I didn't mean to worry you or Cruize or anyone," I stutter as my emotions run havoc on me. I feel incredibly confused now about Maverick, and anxious that people were worried about me. "How did I end up back here in this awful soul-destroying space?" I ponder sadly.

Madison stops cleaning and comes closer, bending down to face me. "That's the problem honey, you block everyone out, but we *want* to help you when you need it. We are your friends. We do not want to make a mad dash, thinking you've been murdered and I'm going to find your mangled body in the house," she states so vividly, swinging her arms around which makes me laugh despite her explanation.

I stop laughing instantly as she glares at me, not impressed with my laughter. "That's a horrible thought Madison, I'm sorry. I promise you I will try and let people in – not of the murdery kind thou." I smile as the tension leaves the room and Madison laughs.

"I mean that," I think to myself, I will try harder. I need to try harder to stop shutting everyone out of my world.

"Good," she replies. "You can't start with filling me in on every single detail about 'Mister—Walking—Sex—God' and what they hell have you two been doing?" She smiles, happy with herself. "And," she continues before I can reply, "after that conversation and a confidence wine, you're going to march over there, talk through this, make up with him, and get over this fight you two had. I'm sure it's something so silly anyways," she states simply as she reaches for the wine in the fridge.

"I'm not so sure he will get over it… Ever," I reply ever so quietly she misses it.

Isabelle

I walk over to Mavericks house, feeling a little happy after two glasses of wine, although I cannot shake my anxiety.

"What if he slams the door in my face? What if he never wants to talk to me ever again? I don't think I could handle that, I already feel as though a part of me is missing without his presence in my life." I sigh as I reach the warehouse steps. I pause and take a breath in before I quietly make my way to the top of the stairs and knock softly on his door.

After what feels like a lifetime of nervous waiting, the door to the warehouse swings open quietly. "It's not Maverick." I breathe a sigh of relief. I think I was going to turn and run if he's still angry at me, my instincts urging me to flee.

"Running has always been my go to. My escape mechanism." I remember that deeply ingrained and inescapable action within me. Although it was Flynn who instilled a different view, a new perspective as he offered his thoughts one dark and stormy night on the island. I recall feeling angry that night, furious I was even on the island, and the reasons that led me there as we watched the lightning strikes illuminate the midnight sky. We listened to the roar of the thunder rumbling in across the island together as he quietly whispered beside me:

"Running is never the answer Isabelle. You've got this – no matter how dark things may seem; the storm will eventually pass." I smile at the memory, in the midst of my own personal storm, he was always my shelter until it passed.

"Well hello young lady, you must be Isabelle." Beams the old man standing in front of me. "Come in sweetheart." He gestures to inside the warehouse as I walk tentatively through the doorway.

"Thank you," I reply nervously. "How did you know?" I add with curiosity.

He laughs, a big bellowing laugh that reminds me of Santa Claus in a way, with his white hair, warm smile and hearty laugh. "Well my dear, Maverick has talked about you before, quite a lot actually." He smiles. "If fact, you're the only person he's ever told me about." He frowns realising what he's just said. "He's outside sleeping love – poor boys got a terrible fever." He shakes his head. "Well, I've got to run to close the store, will you wait with him for a while sweetie?" he asks.

"Sure," I reply smiling politely, not really sure whether I should, or if Maverick will even want me to, but I decide to stay anyways.

"Great, thanks love, I'll see you around soon I hope." He genuinely smiles as he picks up his satchel and heads out the front door, closing it with a gentle click.

I quietly slide the French glass door open and see Maverick lying on the couch. He looks uncomfortable, his eyes are tightly closed, a sheen of sweat dripping down his forehead and his cheeks are blossoming red. I move back inside to fetch a cold towel and a glass of water for him, I have zero experience tending to others but it seems like the right thing to do. I place the cold wet towel on his forehead and feel his cheeks with my fingers, he's burning up and there's nothing I can do to fix him.

I quietly drag one of the sun lounges towards the couch, wanting to be closer to him as I sit upright, waiting in silence.

"He's a beautiful human – inside and out," I think to myself. "Why of all the people on this earth to hurt, it should never have been him," I think sadly. I attempt to work through my muddled thoughts and memorise what I will say to him when he wakes – if he even gives me the opportunity to explain.

Different versions race through my head. "I pride myself on honesty but personal experiences are hard to speak out loud. Especially ones that have a profound impact on you, and your own future. Experiences, you have never spoken aloud." These thoughts weighing heavily on my mind.

I lay back into the sun lounge and close my eyes, feeling the weight of the world upon me. "Just for a second," I think as I drift off into a deep slumber – plagued with doubts.

Maverick

"Isabelle?" I whisper.

I can see her body lying on the sun lounge next to the couch. "She must have fallen asleep." I sigh as I squint, adjusting to the night vision and rubbing my tired eyes, attempting to comprehend what is going on.

I move to sit up slowly and a wet towel falls off my head. "Cute," I quietly whisper to myself. "I think she did that." I ponder as I gaze over at her. Isabelle's hair has fallen over her face and she looks completely at peace in this moment.

"I should let her rest – if she is *actually* is here," I think silently as the couch creaks unexpectedly with my movement. Isabelle's eyes slowly open, although she stays completely still.

"Isabelle?" I ask again, waiting for her to speak so I know I'm not hallucinating this entire scene.

"Hi," she replies quietly. Isabelle moves to sit upright on the sun lounge, which appears to have moved closer to the couch since I have been asleep.

"How long have you been here?" I ask, not even knowing how she got into the warehouse.

"I don't know." She shrugs shyly as she looks down at her feet nervously.

"What do you want?" I ask roughly, which makes her pull away a little further. "I'm sorry," I quickly interject before she can answer. "I didn't mean to snap, I have a throbbing headache and I'm a little confused right now, that's all."

"I came over to talk to you… I wanted to explain Maverick." She looks up at me and then back down at her feet. "A lovely Santa like man let me in, he even knew my name," she explains.

"Yeah, that would be Walter," I reply, staring directly at her, waiting patiently for her to face me again.

"Come here Isabelle," I ask as I extend my hand out to her. She shifts slowly and looks at me but appears somewhat confused or puzzled, perhaps even a little afraid. I never wanted her to be afraid of me. "I told you Isabelle, I'm not going to hurt you, and I never will. Please come here," I plead with her.

I need to feel her.

Isabelle moves towards me and I pull her gently onto my lap. I hug her close to me as she slowly wraps herself around me and moves her hands, massaging them softly through my hair, releasing my boundless tension with her touch.

"God I missed you." I breathe into her ear as she relaxes every bone in my body. She exhales softly, "I think she was holding her breath," I wonder. This would have been understandably hard for her to work up the courage to come here. I know her default mechanism is 'running' from what I can surmise and ultimately avoiding talking about anything difficult.

"Okay Isabelle, I'm listening," I whisper in her ear as I move to kiss her on the cheek gently and release her from our embrace. I move her across my lap to face me with her legs comfortably balanced across mine. I lean forward, running my hand across her chin and sweeping her hair back away from her face.

"This, would want to be the best god damn explanation I've ever heard in my life," I silently seethe to myself. I can't handle the thought of anyone, let alone someone as special as her, tried to take their own life.

She fidgets with her own hands, twisting them anxiously

together as she thinks. Isabelle takes a deep breath before she speaks. "Mav, I meant what I said to you, it's not what you think. I've just never had to explain it before to anyone," she starts. "But I want to explain it to you."

I don't speak, whatever I have to say right now is not fucking nice. My thoughts are filled with a slow burning anger with the intensity of a wildfire and my head is pounding relentlessly so I remain silent and slowly nod at her in response.

"So, it was about two years ago, maybe more I'm not sure. A lot of my memories are cloudy or hard to recall. Maverick you need to understand that. It's my brain protecting me I think." She pauses and takes another breath. "This is really hard for her," I realise painfully as I nod and pull her hands into mine, carefully avoiding her wrists but running my fingers gently along hers.

"It was raining outside that night; I remember as it had been raining for the past three or four days non-stop and the roads were dangerous. I wasn't thinking clearly, I was driving home from work around eleven p.m. that night." She explains quietly. "I took the forest roads, I thought it would be better than the highway. I couldn't see the lines dividing the lanes on the highway, it was almost impossible as the heavy rain continuously pelted my windshield."

She pauses and looks up at me to gain a reaction, I simply nod again, not letting my vexed emotions escape as she continues.

"I was crying while I was driving. I had experienced a very rough couple of months and I was both physically and emotionally exhausted. I cried every day and all night. I was wiping my face, trying to focus on the road but I could barely see, the rain was too heavy, and the windscreen wipers didn't seem to be working against the onslaught of the rain," she whispers as her fingers intertwine with mine and a tear rolls down her face.

"I flicked the high beam lights on in the car, but it was too late. In the middle of the forest road, deep in the gully was a fallen tree. I slammed on the brakes as hard as I could, I always thought not to swerve in these types of situations so I held the steering tight and the wheels locked up." More tears roll down her face as she recalls this moment.

I pull my hand up and cup her face to wipe her tears away. God this girl really blows my mind, she's so fucking beautiful and yet so broken. I wish I could fix her. I would do anything to see her smile. I would walk barefoot to the ends of the earth just to take her pain away right now. This is not what I expected at all, but my anger is still taunting me just below the surface.

"I knew I was going to crash, but I thought I would hit the fallen tree head on and the airbags would activate. I was so stupid; I locked the wheels up and the car skidded in the wet. It was sliding across the road so fast I didn't know which way I was facing," she explains. I pull her closer and kiss her cheek, this is not the explanation I was expecting as I feel my anger slowly subsiding, being replaced with a deep feeling of hurt. I feel like I've been violently stabbed and the knife is twisting painfully in my gut with every word she recalls.

"The car slammed side on into another tree down the embankment. The airbags didn't activate, there was no side airbags, only front collision airbags." She exhales and slowly continues. "I smashed my head on the window upon impact so I must have been out of it." She lifts her hair slowly to uncover another scar on her temple. I run my fingers down it, tracing the scar with the tips of my fingers as she lets her hair fall back down.

I'm lost for words right now. What could I possibly say in this moment to understand. To be in that moment and take her pain? Nothing. I feel my insides tearing apart with the pain and horror she must have felt as she experienced this, and my regret as I judged her without actually listening first. Without being there to support her and now forcing her to unburden this secret to me – I really fucking hate myself right now.

"The emergency services must have been en route by the time I awoke from the impact as I could just make out the blurry red and blue lights, they were flashing wildly in the distance through darkness of the forest. I moved and released my seatbelt and scrambled out of the driver's window and onto the wet grass," she continues. "I got up and ran," she states as she looks me dead in the eye.

I don't understand that part as I slowly wipe her tears and question: "Isabelle, why would you run?" I prompt, unsure I want to even know the answer, but she is here and vulnerable and I'm willing to listen. I'm not a complete asshole and I understand real torment when I see it.

"Maverick I ran, and I kept running. I put my hands up to protect my face as there were so many trees and branches scratching... cutting me everywhere. The forest was so thick and I was completely lost in the dark amidst the storm. I pushed through the branches with my hands, it was some kind of thicket blanketed with thorns that I had become trapped in and it cut deep into my wrists and hands. My boots and jeans protected my legs, my jacket protected my arms and I protected my face with my hands. I tore free of the thorns and I knew I was bleeding heavily but I just kept running until there was no more left in me. I ran and kept running until I eventually collapsed on the forest floor on the wet ground," she sobs.

"Isabelle, why would you hide your scars if you didn't do this to yourself intentionally?" I ask slowly. Isabelle looks away from me. "I haven't finished the story yet Maverick," she replies softly. "I was found much later, almost dead from bleeding out, I ran so far the emergency services said it was a fight or flight response due to a traumatic experience." She starts to shiver and I pull her close.

I want to squeeze every single drop of this experience out of her and fucking kill it. I don't speak. I don't know what to say. I want to take her pain away. I'm still angry as I feel the flames pulse through my veins, but not at her. Just angry at the world, the rain, the car, the tree – all of it unreasonable. I reflect in this moment, how entirely fucked up the universe is; I've found someone who has stolen my heart and fucking owns me completely, simply by just being her – although we can never be, there will be no happy ending for us.

"Maverick, I hide the scars because there too painful for me to look at. I didn't want to wake up that night of the accident, I wanted to make my pain go away. I was so angry when I had come too after the accident, so very angry." Isabelle takes moment and glances up into the night sky. "Maverick I was angry that I had been saved. I wasn't worth saving." She breathes in almost a furious whisper. "What for I wanted to know? Why me? There are millions of other people in the world who are worth saving – so much more than me. Why did they have to save me? I didn't deserve it. I was so angry I ran, and I ran and I just kept running until I blacked out," she whispers.

"Maverick I didn't want to wake up. Ever." She sobs in my arms.

My body is racked with pain, the jagged knife now twisting deeper, this time directly into my heart. She's so incredibly beautiful, intelligent and a rare special gift to the universe, yet she is so broken, and damaged through the trials she has faced on her own perilous journey. I finally understand a tiny glimmer of what she is and what she has been through. I want to fucking murder the people who made her feel like this. I'm so angry my body feels like it's burning in the deepest depths of hell. I want to start tearing the warehouse down piece by piece, I want to scream, I want to fight with every last breath I have, and I want to hunt down these fuckers that hurt her. I don't know who did this, but I do know – I will find out, and when I do – every single motherfucker is going to pay for hurting her.

I'm so tense my muscles ache. I can't breathe considering this and every implication of what she has just said, although I need to contain my emotions. I know she doesn't need an out of control wildfire right now. My intense anger and furious emotions will only add fuel to this bonfire – she needs a gentle rain and I want to be the rain, her rain. I want to be a shelter for her and every instinct I have is telling me to fiercely protect her.

"If only she knew." Thoughts race through my head about my own secrets I keep from her. "I can never tell her now," I think to myself.

She cannot know.

Ever.

Isabelle

"I will understand if you never speak to me again Maverick, I just wanted to explain it to you." I turn and tell him slowly as I wipe my tears away.

It's done now. I laid my soul bare to one of the darkest moments I had ever experienced and now the rest is up to him. I know I hurt him. I can tell he is hurting but his silence is worse than his anger. I have to speak slowly or I'm at risk of losing all self-control, my emotions are raw and my body is fragile. I feel like I could snap with the slightest draft of wind heading my way.

I'm exhausted and an emotional wreck after reliving this experience, a moment I had buried so deep within my mind – firmly locked inside the vault. I can't believe I'm here explaining my life to him – "Again, another rule of mine broken." I think quietly to myself as I slowly release my hands from Mavericks and stand up, turning to walk back through the balcony doors.

"I can't be here. I need to leave," I think sadly as I walk back towards the front entrance, further away from a very still and silent Maverick.

"Isabelle… wait," he shouts from the outdoor couch. I stop in my tracks; his voice makes my heart stutter with a tiny sliver of hope.

I am absolutely devastated I hurt him. I feel so broken and I am entirely lost, it is like wandering in the dark when you can't find the light switch – you know it's there – but have no idea how to find it in the pitch blackness.

I am not sure why I even pursued this. He makes me happy with the simplest of things, yet here I am, completely screwing life up again. I've made him angry, he is sick, and here I am unburdening horrible truths. "I am an awful human," I breathe quietly.

"Isabelle, please come back," he shouts again, interrupting my negative thoughts.

"I owe you a lesson." I can hear the smile in his voice.

I step back through the door and stare incredulous at him. "Sorry, what did you say?" I ask, shocked at his calmer nonchalant attitude.

"I said," he states quite loudly in his beautiful deep voice, "Miss Perfect, I owe you a lesson. Remember – you master the chords and I learn something about you. Your *way* ahead right now and I haven't taught you anything." He smirks and winks as he scoots up on the couch.

The goddess Aphrodite urges me forward in my mind as desire pulses through me, his voice and body triggering a riot in my thoughts. He is incredibly attractive when he's not angry at the world and instead; turns his passion into charm. His muscles peep through his shirt and I can see his intricate tattoos snaking up his arm as he plays with his lip ring, twirling it within his fingers while he waits for my answer.

I think he enjoys it when I'm rendered speechless by him. My whole body reacts to him and I believe he can sense it as he returns a playful smile and holds out his hand for me to come to him.

"Maverick," I say slowly and purposefully. "I think you should walk away from me now." I state honestly as he peers at me with a look of hurt and confusion.

"Why?" he demands as he moves and stands up.

"Maverick, I'm not what you need. I'm damaged goods. I am scarred and not good for you," I state. This is tearing me apart. I feel like my legs will collapse at any moment, and my heart is screaming a resounding 'no!'… but I need to let him go.

He moves quickly towards me, closing the space between us as he places his hands around my waist and pulls me tightly towards him. He rests his forehead against my mine and he doesn't speak for what feels like a lifetime. I can feel his heartbeat and I sense his tension, intricately wound deep into his muscles but I cannot feel his mind; his thoughts and emotions elude me. "I wish I knew what he was thinking right now," as a million heavy thoughts ricochet wildly through my head.

"Isabelle," he states gently. "Isabelle, I want to be here for you as long as I can. I will wait as long as you need, until you are ready. I will walk to the end of universe just to make sure no one hurts you, ever again," he whispers as bends down and kisses my forehead.

Unspoken minutes pass, and just for a moment, a tender moment, I feel happy. I feel blissfully content, as in this very moment; there is no drama, no anger, no past, no future – just simply us with an overwhelming sense of peace as he wraps his powerful arms around me. He smells of embers and storms, it is intoxicating as it embodies the very essence of him. The danger within the fire, the darkness of the night and the menace within the storm – all an enchantment of him.

"Mav, you don't even truly know me." My heart cracks as I eventually reply and release myself from him, attempting to walk away. I need to let him go. "He is like gold," I think to myself, "a precious element to be carefully treasured," I reflect. "He deserves a diamond, someone with clarity and strength, someone who illuminates his world."

He doesn't let go. "Isabelle, don't," he pleads. "Don't go."

"Why Maverick, why do you want me to stay?" I whisper.

"I just seem to make you angry and sad. You lash out when your hurt and that's because of me," I elaborate sadly. "I don't want that for you Maverick. I *never* wanted that for you," I enunciate slowly.

He backs down towards the couch, releasing my hand and places his head softly in between his hands. I stand immobile, frozen in place. "Am I breaking up with someone I'm not even in a relationship with?" I think to myself. "Do I really want this?" questions race through me. "What am I doing?" I consider, silently praying that Flynn has some words of wisdom for me in this exact moment.

Maverick sits on the couch motionless as I slowly take a tentative step closer and he puts his hand out to stop me. "Don't," he states sadly as he continues.

"Isabelle, I've made a lot of mistakes. A fuckload of mistakes. I've been an asshole and I've...." he pauses. "Well let's say I can't take back the things I've done," he whispers as I try again to move closer to him, slowly bending down in front of him when he makes no attempt to stop me this time.

I'm hurting him and his pain is contagious. I breathe in and out deeply, attempting to slow my heart and quiet my mind while I wait. Needing to hear – what is within his heart, and what is troubling his mind.

"Isabelle, I want to tear the people apart who fucking hurt you. I want to tear them to pieces, just as they have torn you apart. It makes me so fucking wild with anger but I'm so sorry if I ever made you afraid of me," he states honestly as he looks at me, staring with his dark eyes. Maverick runs his hand through his messy dark hair and grabs me by the waist gently.

"You are my world right now Isabelle, today – fuck, you are my god dam world every day, every hour, every minute, every second. Your *all* I think about, and you're certainly the light in my chaotic dark world." My heart stutters with his revelations.

"I can't tell you everything, but I promise you with everything I have left – I will never hurt you. I want to protect you… and I never wanted you to be afraid of me," he pleads.

I'm so conflicted, all the promises I made to myself that I'm breaking, simply by letting him in. And all the unknowns with trying not to hurt him with my own inner turmoil, leaves me jumbled, like the pieces of an unfinished puzzle.

"It's okay to let people in. You need to know that Belle, you need to believe that." Flynn chants in my head. "No. Set him free. He deserves it." I promise myself unconvincingly.

"I've never been afraid of you Maverick." I start slowly, gathering my thoughts. "My only fear is that you would, and have completely stolen my heart. I know I gave it to you willingly though; tiny piece by piece to keep safe and protected with you always, hidden within your armour. Although I also know – you are so much better than this and you certainly deserve better than me." I plea with him, hoping he lets me go – as I sure as hell know I cannot let him go right now, my resolve to leave slowly stuttering and making its own escape.

"Your all I need Isabelle," he states confidently as he moves and grabs my face with both his hands. "Your all I want." He places his forehead on mine and I close my eyes, embracing him. He makes me feel as though I have just taken my whole heart out of my chest and handed it to him willingly. Although, I already know, I have been giving tiny fragments of my heart to him since the very first moment I heard him, knowing he would keep them safe.

"I need to let this beautiful person go but I just don't know if I am strong enough." I wrestle with this as he moves his hand to my chin and pulls my face closer to his. He's so incredibly close to my lips – I sense all of him. I can smell his fragrance, I can feel him and my body is calling for him as he pulls me closer. "Tell me 'no' Isabelle," he whispers and then places his lips gently on mine, ever so slowly.

My body tingles at the touch of his lips on mine. I don't want him to stop as he kisses me so passionately and intimately. I feel his heartbeat, his wishes and his desire. Mavericks hands delicately roam with his breath on my cheek. Our embrace is something so impossible, so beautiful, I would give up the world to stay here as long as possible, an everlasting moment. He's broken my entire resolve with one kiss. "I don't want you to stop Maverick," I whisper as I move my lips to his cheek and slowly trail kisses down his neck. Maverick groans and then grabs me under my arms and pulls me swiftly to my feet. He turns and walks forwards as I step backwards until my back is against the wall, returning the kisses down my face and neck. His hands continue to roam my face and body. He is entirely dangerous, yet so gentle and perfectly in control, he knows what he wants completely and it is so natural it drives me wild with desire. "Isabelle," he groans loudly as he moves his body closer to connect with mine against the wall. "Tell me what you want, I don't want to control myself around you," he whispers as he trails kisses down my neck and his hands gently caress me. "Maverick," I breathe. "I want you," I whisper.

He wastes not a second as he lifts me swiftly, not taking his lips from mine as he carries me to his bedroom.

Isabelle

He's perched on a stool next to the bed, his acoustic guitar within his hands, poised for a minute of thought as I rub my eyes softly. "Am I dreaming?" I think to myself. The most unique and incredible man is sitting not two metres away from me. Maverick is shirtless, just his trademark black ripped jeans and a studded dark leather belt covering his perfectly sculpted body. "I'm the luckiest woman in the world right now." I smile to myself.

I silently inspect him; his body is defined, his muscles are easily distinguishable by the way he's sitting and holding his guitar, his abs are chiselled and a tattoo weaves up his right side.

"Mavericks tattoo appears to be some sort of scripture written in Persian or Egyptian hieratic perhaps?" I wonder curiously about this as I gaze at the detailed ink, it wraps around his ribs with what appears to be a dragon, weaving menacingly around the scripture. His dark jet-black hair washes over his face as he stares down at the strings on his guitar. He strums slowly, bringing a genuine smile to my face and I know in that moment – I want to watch him play for a bit longer. "A lifetime perhaps." I wildly dream.

I open my eyes again when he starts to play, unable to stop myself as I listen intently whilst he strums. The rhythm sounds like 'Big White Room' but I can't be sure. It's so haunting yet unexpectedly beautiful. Every time he plays it touches me deep within my soul. My body shivers with the energy he places into every note, every word, every expression as I feel silent tears of an unfathomable peace well gently within my eyes.

Listening to him play is haunting. "He is haunted by something. I just can't place it yet," I consider.

He looks up and stops playing, he slowly places his guitar against the stool and comes over to the side of the bed. I sit up and move the sheets to my chest. "Hi" I smile at him nervously. "I bet I look like I have risen from the depths of hell right now," I scream in my head. He doesn't smile back. "Did I hurt you Isabelle?" he asks.

Well… that wasn't a question I was expecting after the wonderful night we just experienced together. Every single one of my senses is on high alert, wanting him, needing him again. "Huh, Sorry?" I reply surprised at the first words that come out of his mouth. I am utterly confused. "Why are you crying Isabelle? You have tears in your eyes?" he urges as he stares at me concerned.

I can't drag my eyes off his beautiful body (as wildly inappropriate thoughts invade my mind). Although my rational brain understands he is serious, his tone worried. I push my scandalous thoughts away I sit up further and grab his face softly with my hands. I can honestly say, this man is more beautiful in both heart and mind than I ever imagined.

"Mav, I'm sorry I'm not crying and I'm most certainly not hurt. Every song you play is so unimaginably beautiful. It reaches every sense in my body, touches my emotions in ways not even I can understand, I cannot help but respond to your magical sound." I smile as the tension leaves Mavericks expression. "You are truly remarkable," I whisper as I kiss his lips. He sighs in relief, I think, I hope.

"Hmm." He shrugs his shoulders and chuckles.

"What are you doing today songbird?" he asks as he kisses my forehead. "Umm… well I've got a photo shoot for my job today, so I will be in the park first and then I need to visit a few local businesses." I reply excited for my next work assignments.

"It will take me a few hours to capture the images of each business then after that I have no plans," I reply lazily as I raise my arms above my head to stretch my entire body.

"I've got a few hours before I have to go in though." I smirk with an eyebrow raise. "So anything come to mind? I'm all ears?" I smile with the boldness of my statement. "Holy shit, did I really just say that out loud?" I cringe, horrified in my head. "God I'm such a ridiculously embarrassing human and I know Flynn is laughing out loud right now as his lessons in life went completely out the window where Maverick is concerned."

I'm silently cursing myself as Maverick releases the buckle on his belt with a wicked smile as he joins me back in bed.

Maverick

I need to see Walter. "I need advice," I encourage myself as I push open the door to the music shop.

"Hi Maverick." Walter smiles as he places down the piece he was working on. "Hey Walter, how are you?" I reply nonchalantly although my mind is anything but.

Fuck, this is hard; I've never spoken to anyone about my feelings. Ever. Arizona would be the exception but we barely scratch the surface of my complicated mind.

"Walter, I was wondering if you could help me with something?" I ask sheepishly.

"Sure Mav, what do you need?" he enquires as he raises his eyebrow in question, peering over at me. I've never asked for anything from Walter so he probably assuming the worst as I stumble through my words.

"I need… no, I mean I *want* to do something nice for someone, something that speaks volumes that I can't say out loud." My voice fails to express the feelings I have. "Fuck this is crazy, I have known her less than a year, but I would do absolutely anything for her. I consider my dramatic thoughts and the extent I would go to for her; walking across hot coals taken from burning the ashes of Pompeii to get to her, hand digging her a diamond out of the Mir mine in Siberia to jousting Sir Galahad in ancient times to prove the strength of my armour – everything to protect her and anything to make her happy." I consider this as I realise the extent of my feelings for her. Walter interrupts my confusing, titanic sized thoughts as I prepare to willingly throw myself off my own ship as I am completely at her mercy.

"Mav, I will help you of course. You know you already have the words – you just don't know how to express them yet. Would this something be for a certain Isabelle?" He smiles broadly.

His words mean more than he knows. I have a deep ache in my soul, threatening to erupt like a volcano as I know that without a shred of doubt; I am going to cause her pain eventually. I never wanted to be someone to hurt her, but the closer we become, the more I can't let her go right now, nor ever. I know she is going to be fucking devastated when she finds out what I'm hiding and why I'm hiding it, not just from her but the entire fucking world. The universe is a straight-up asshole.

I am also a complete fucking asshole not letting her go, I know this. Her presence and her spirit are what's keeping me going each day, so yes – I am being entirely selfish wanting to keep her, when I already know I cannot. A better man would have let her go, not pursued her knowing that this will not end happily.

"Yeah Walter, it's for her." I smile as I run my hands through my hair and stuff them back in my jean pockets, observing the ground beneath me. I can pour my heart out on stage through song but expressing emotions in this way is something entirely different. Something unfamiliar and completely foreign to me.

Walter helps me plan something for Isabelle. I want nothing more than to see her smile. She's so naively innocent and hurt. It's absolutely mystifying to me that any human being would even want to intentionally hurt her, she's an extraordinary, kind and beautiful person. Isabelle illuminates even the darkest room with her aura and walks her own path as free spirit, "and she does it all in her absurd magenta boots." I smile to myself at the memory of the first time I spotted her, marching through the bar in those boots.

Isabelle has shown me life can be pure and brought me a sense of peace I never, ever thought was possible. That is a priceless gift in itself she has given me – she walked into my life when I needed it the most; when I was devastatingly lost and completely wandering alone, on a journey that has no way home.

Maverick

I walk over to Isabelle's after her shift for the magazine and knock lightly on the door. An unfamiliar car is parked in the driveway, although Isabelle didn't mention any plans for this afternoon. She asked me to come around to see her latest pictures for an upcoming cover story she was asked to provide the artwork for. After a few minutes of waiting with no answer, I make my way around back of the property. "I know sometimes she reads out at the back patio after work to relax, or maybe she's down at lake and simply cannot hear the door," I consider this to myself.

I spot her standing near the water as I round the back of the house. Isabelle's family home is magnificent, with a full lush garden that borders the paths and compliments the intricate whitewash timber planks on the boardwalk as they lead you down towards the placid lake, complete with their own family jetty. We lay out on the jetty on warm nights and simply look up at the stars together. Isabelle finds most things we take for granted an inspiring gift that we all should treasure. It really gives you another refreshing perspective on life when you look at the world through her lens, something I never thought was possible – Ever. When you take moment to pause, reflect and truly appreciate what you have (no matter how short that may be), what you have experienced (no matter how painful that may be), it can open your eyes, your mind, and (fucking unbelievable to me) your heart to the very impossible – hope.

A short drive through the main street of this small town and you are standing on the beach, the ocean lapping at your feet and the warm sand in between your toes. I observed the wonder and beauty this town had to offer when I first arrived, although I find with the more time I spend here – there is always another precious jewel to be unearthed. The places here are hidden away, untroubled and utterly captivating which always leaves me speechless in its wake. There have been so many times I've wanted to also share these special places with Arizona. I know she would truly appreciate them, but I made a promise to myself a long time ago, deciding that staying away was the best choice in this fucked-up situation.

I spot Isabelle, her hands-on-hips facing someone I don't recognise. Her long blonde hair is billowing in the wind. She moves her hands, clenching them tightly together in front of her and twisting them as she stares up directly at the stranger.

He's tall, dark short cropped hair, military style and distastefully dressed in some kind of bomber jacket and chinos. I have never seen him before, "Perhaps he's not a local?" I wonder as I approach slowly.

I don't take my eyes of Isabelle on my approach, she looks like she's crying from a distance as she uses her hands to wipe her eyes. Anger rises up in me immediately like a volcano rising to the surface, the heat of the lava bubbles emerge in sync with my heart as it beats faster, and faster. I burn with rage at the very thought of someone, anyone at all – hurting her again. I stomp towards them with the force of battalion as she places her head in her hands and shakes her head in front of him.

He grabs her arms as he moves closer to her and she attempts to shake him off. "Don't fucking touch her!" I roar as I approach the two of them.

"Who are you?" he states as he turns slightly to face me without letting her go.

"None of your business asshole, now leave her alone. It is obvious she does not appreciate you touching her," I state flatly as I move closer.

"Izzy. Who the fuck is this?" he demands as he turns back to face her.

She removes her hands from her face and looks between the two of us, her face stained with tears. My heart sinks. "This fucking bastard thinks it's okay to make her cry? I'm fucking furious," I seethe silently.

"Izzy babe, we need to talk, let's go inside." He speaks directly to her, completely ignoring me as he moves his hands from her arms and grabs her wrist, lightly tugging her towards the house. I would recognise this as an attempt at controlling her. "This is not going to go well for him if he thinks control is the way through to her," I think rationally to myself. "This guy has no idea and if he touches her again, I will fucking kill him." I decide without hesitation, consequences be dammed.

"Don't touch me Elijah. You have no right," she whispers angrily as she swiftly yanks her wrist from his hands.

A fire rips through me, "Elijah? the one who gives her nightmares? I'm going to murder this motherfucker," I think to myself, hardly able to contain my anger. She won't speak a word of him but I know he must have had something to do with her pain and her scars.

Isabelle interrupts my out of control train of angry thoughts, her voice shaky. "Elijah. We have nothing to talk about and I need you to leave now," she states firmly as she points to the front of the house. "Izzy baby, I said I was sorry. I made a mistake, please don't do this," he begs.

I feel like I'm watching an old movie, one of those black and white ones where it's a bit staticky and lines blur through the screen as I struggle to reconcile this situation. I'm so fired up and very fucking angry, all I can think about is inflicting pain upon him and the million different ways I want to do it. I want to make him hurt a billion times worse than her hurt her.

My rational brain slowly intercepts my train wreck of 'ways to annihilate him' as I realise, "fuck, I can't be the one in control here, I need her to do this for herself. She always talks about becoming a stronger version of herself and if I interfere now I know she won't be thankful for it. Although, the minute he takes another step or lays so much as a finger on her I will literally kill him, so for Isabelle's sake." I think to myself, "I'm praying this fuckwit stays put."

"Elijah, I'm a different person now. I've learnt so much from you, but I'm not the girl you once knew. I've grown, I'm stronger and importantly, I am happy without you." She sighs and looks down to her feet.

"She does that when she's nervous," I remember and I've only known her a short while. "Surely this guy can understand he's making her fucking anxious right now?" I think angrily.

She slowly looks up at him and continues, "You've taught me how not to treat a person, you've taught me the difference between right and wrong in a relationship, and you were most definitely in the wrong. You taught me the difference between love and dependency, and most of all you've taught me to become a stronger person. I'm not the person you once knew and you need to leave. You've made your choices and I've made mine," she adds shakily.

He scoffs. "Izzy, your being dramatic, we are meant to be together. I'm sorry, how many times do you need to hear it?

Everyone goes through problems in their relationships. Don't tell me you're with this guy?" he adds as he points to me while still staring at her. "You are so much better than this Izzy?" He finishes.

I curl my fist into a ball and clench my teeth so tight. "This guy is a complete jerk. What an utterly bullshit attempt at an apology if I ever heard one," I fume silently when her voice interrupts me. "Elijah, he's more of a man than you will ever be, he's honest, kind and most of all he sees the person I am, not the person you want me to be. I could never be what you wanted me to be." Her eyes well up with tears again.

"Now go Elijah, there is nothing here for you," she finishes.

I'm so fucking proud of her. I want to go to her, comfort her and tell her she's fucking incredible, but I restrain as he leans in closer to whisper in her ear. She flinches as he gets closer until he stops and it looks like she is holding her breath at his proximity. "Your nothing without me Isabelle. Your dead to me," he whispers to her, although I catch the entire sentence and can longer stand back and watch him treat her like this. "This deadbeat needs to remove himself entirely from her life, and my presence before I assault him and throw him in a ditch he cannot dig his way out of," I think before I react. I'm rational, (very fucking angry but semi rational, let's be honest) as I actually gave this guy a chance to explain himself – but this fucker just snapped my very thin line of patience and understanding. There is no way in this entire universe I would ever speak to a woman like that, and I snap.

I swing my arm back swiftly and sharply, the blow landing directly on the side of his face and right across his nose. I feel the intense pain as it connects with his face and ripples back through my knuckles, continuing up my arm and into my shoulder.

I'm so fucking wound up. I could beat him, and just keep beating him to release all of the anger I feel right now, attempting to reduce the loathing I have for him. And the entire world for that fact if I truly reflect on what this is.

The pain he has inflicted upon her is my pain. My manic anger is running rampant within me, united with a monumental 'fuck you' from the universe – sadly I feel as though everyone is celebrating in my head with a big win, although I feel defeated. "The defeat you feel when you know it has won. The moment you know the world has kicked you while you were down for the final time and there is no more fight left in you," I consider this to myself. "Why the fuck is everything a test, some fucking challenge to test your absolute limits?" I ask myself angrily.

The intense rage I'm feeling right now at what he has done, and what I have done, is all consuming. My head is fucking pounding and I have the feeling of fire running right through my veins. "However, no matter how angry I am," I seethe to myself as I think of my sister and my mother. "No woman should ever in their life have to experience this." I reflect as my mother and father instilled the very best morals in Arizona and I growing up. We were taught that everyone is equal, you respect each other, you help those in need and importantly – protect and defend each other, although always remember, you do not have the right to intentionally hurt someone else.

I consider my parents advice, knowing that no matter how persistent my mind is, urging me with an evil hand to rid the earth of this piece of shit bleeding on the ground – I refuse to fight anyone who is not capable or already down and out.

He takes a moment to compose himself while these rapid thoughts barrel through my head and Isabelle stands silently.

Elijah wipes the blood from his nose with the back of his hand. I instinctively move to stand protectively in between Isabelle and him whilst he pushes himself slowly off the ground and stands back up. I don't know if this guy is a loose cannon but I certainly don't trust him anywhere near Isabelle. He spits on the ground at my feet, turning abruptly to march off back towards the front of the house. Elijah leave silently without a word as the adrenaline starts to recede within me.

The pounding in my head grows louder and more painful with every breath, eventually I know I can no longer stand as my knees hit the ground hard. The darkness wins as it aggressively takes control and cripples me. I groan and finally surrender, feeling my entire body succumb as I hit the grass sharply.

I vaguely hear his car speed off, the tyres skidding in the gravel out of the driveway as I yield to the pain.

Isabelle

"Maverick!" I scream as he lies helplessly on the grass.

"Mav, please answer me?" I panic. He appears to be pain; his face is flushed and body curled into a tight fetal position.

His eyes blink awake, dark and fearsome. "What is wrong with him?" I panic to myself as tears stream down my face. All the emotions of today have erupted out of me, my tears fall like cascading water droplets from the peak of the highest waterfall. He makes no attempt to move after a few quiet moments so I lay down beside him as he lies stricken on the grass. I creep closer and lay my head gently on his chest, I don't know what else to do. "Maverick please tell me you are okay," I whisper.

"Isabelle," he replies quietly after a few minutes. I'm instantly more alert, my tears halt their silent storm and I sit up and move my ear closer to his lips. "Isabelle, help me inside please," he breathes.

I help Maverick inside the house, not without a struggle. He's incredibly heavy with his muscle weight and I don't think I can take much credit for 'helping' as there is no way I can support his body weight on my own. We move silently and slowly inside to the couch in front of the fire as he lays down and closes his eyes once again. "Can I get you anything?" I whisper. Maverick slowly motions a 'no' with his head although holds out his hand for me, beckoning me closer. I move carefully in beside him on the couch and place my arms around his waist. I pull a blanket gently over us as I softly lay my head on his chest.

I listen intently as Mavericks heartbeat evens out slowly and he quickly falls asleep, his chest rising and falling in a peaceful rhythm.

I lay awake for hours beside him, one million dreadful thoughts blazing through my head while he rests. My thoughts become progressively more negative as the hours pass. "I am a walking disaster and I knew somewhere deep inside me, the very first time I heard him play – that the universe wouldn't let me be happy, it wouldn't let him stay." I ponder this sadly, coming to the conclusion that it is not the universe that will drive him away; ultimately I now understand – it is *me* that will drive him away.

My head hurts with these unhappy thoughts as I close my eyes and wait for him to rise – and walk away forever.

Isabelle

"Isabelle?" he breathes as he opens his eyes.

"I'm here Maverick," I reply as I run my hand down his cheek in a soft embrace. I'm praying silently that he makes this quick. Like ripping off a band aid, but instead of a band aid – I know it will be my entire heart he rips out and takes with him as he walks away.

Everyone leaves.

"Isabelle, are you okay? Is he gone?" he replies softly. He's unusually calm. I know Maverick operates on a different level to me completely, simply by observing his actions and reactions. He can go from zero to a hundred instantly – fired up ready to take on the world at the slightest infraction. These triggers have nothing to do with me... I would like to believe.

I feel unreservedly safe and protected in his presence always, without question. He is always looking for some unknown threat – something to be taken down and taken care of. I visualise it like a demon menacing on his shoulder, waiting to strike at the most opportune moment. Whilst the threat has indeed left, the demon lingers, unable to be moved like a gargoyle, intimidating every person who attempts to get even remotely close to him.

I'm terribly haunted by my own past, yet Maverick does not share *his* demons, ever. I get an awful inkling that perhaps his demons are winning the fight he wages internally each day. "It appears the fight is exhausting him...it seems to drain the energy, light, and very life out of him with every passing day," I observe.

Maverick battles with whatever haunts him and I know I am entirely not helping with the chaos that appears to follow me relentlessly. No matter how hard I try to dig (and dig) myself out of the mayhem that is me – I cannot seem to escape it. "I never wanted Maverick to be faced with any of this," I think sadly.

"You're not responsible for the happiness of those around you Isabelle." Flynn chimes in my ear as I remember him telling me that on a starlight night, although it feels wrong now. I am responsible for this and the pain I have caused Maverick.

Maverick has been my soul, my heart and my entire happiness for so long now. It feels like our souls have known each other a whole lifetime, like a magnet reconnecting that *always* should have been connected. He gets me completely – my scars are his scars and he has never once; asked me to change, expected me to change or judged the journey I took to become the person I am today – no matter how imperfect I am. He sees through the facade and sees the person I am and the person I will become.

I feel as though destiny or perhaps fate brought us together. We were meant to collide on our journey. "Although it is more apparent that my destiny could actually be within the hands of the devil; Lucifer himself who likes to taunt me with 'the idea' of what I 'could have' but 'will never have'." I think negatively about this, weighing my own heart and soul against the ancient Egyptian scales with the goddess of truth. Our relationship is absolutely nothing like what I had with Elijah, or anyone else for that matter. Ever. Although the goddess of truth haunts me relentlessly as I cannot bring myself to explain my pain, and my life 'before' Maverick. He has stolen my heart entirely and kept it safe within his own citadel every day since. "Why should I burden him with my past?" I consider.

I have never experienced life with anyone in the way I do with Maverick. Every single experience is exclusively unique and special. The very thought of him walking away crushes my soul beyond recognition, even though I promised myself a very long time ago – that no man will ever be allowed beyond the fortress walls I built around my heart. Maverick has done precisely that, and broken through the heavy blockade to my heart. This is exactly where I did not want to be again – vulnerable and opening myself up to the possibility of being hurt.

"You may fall down on your journey Isabelle, and that's okay because you are strong. You will pick yourself up, learn those lessons and try again." Flynn pushes into my memories.

"He's gone Mav. I'm so sorry" I whisper.

"Are you going to tell me about Elijah now?" Maverick asks quietly as he opens his eyes and shifts on the couch. He quietly moves, sitting a little more upright and shuffling the cushions behind his back.

"Didn't you see enough Maverick? Why do I need to replay every horrible detail of my life to you?" I sigh dejectedly.

I'm not happy about this and it's apparent in my voice, however he doesn't reply for a few moments. His dark eyes bore straight into me as we sit silently together.

"Isabelle, I come over to see you and there is some guy standing there – with you clearly upset. I'm not a rocket scientist; but I can only assume he hurt you in some way, he caused you pain and he is one of the reasons for your scars. All of this makes me very fucking angry," he states matter of fact. "I'm so proud of you today, so very proud Isabelle." He continues, "but I want you to let me in. I don't want to hear 'every horrible detail' as you describe it, but I want to know you Isabelle, the *real* you."

Maverick places his hand over mine and pulls me gently back towards him. I embrace him as we lay interconnected together in silence, his patience in abundance in this moment whilst I gather my thoughts.

That is entirely not the answer I was expecting. I take a moment to put my heart back in my chest as I absorb everything he has just said. Even with his kind words, I still don't want to talk about any of this. "Bottling it all up, sealing the lid and throwing the jar into the deepest, darkest depths of the ocean – will work better for everyone," I think to myself.

"Isabelle." He interrupts my thoughts. "I will never intentionally hurt you. I would burn down the entire fucking world to make sure you never shed another single unhappy tear. I'm not perfect, fuck, very far from it, but know that I am here for you, for as long as I can be and as long as you'll let me be." Maverick whispers those words as he closes his eyes and lays his head back on the couch, falling back into a deep sleep.

Isabelle

The sun sets slowly on the day. A vivid sunset display of oranges and reds over the pristine lake. I watch the lake shimmer through the expanse windows overlooking the water as I begin to shift beside Maverick whilst he sleeps soundly. We spent the afternoon simply wrapped closely together in a contented silence, cocooned protectively in each other's arms.

I needed time to process my kaleidoscope of thoughts. Process everything that happened with Elijah, and truly consider the significance of Mavericks words today. Although, as the hours pass – I still don't have any answers for Maverick. My ability to open up and communicate is a big black void, I don't even know where to begin. My brain ticks into overdrive and my anxiety surges if I even attempt to consider telling Maverick about my past... and what haunts me.

"I should prepare my photos for the magazine that I took today." I sigh. I feel equally awake, yet exhausted which is difficult to reconcile. My mind is completely alive and restless with these numerous jumbled thoughts, although my body is lifeless. It feels as though my limbs are made of lead as I attempt to get up off the couch and finish my submission for the editors.

I make my way down to the study quietly, careful not wake Maverick as I collect my camera from my satchel. I fire up the computer and wait to scan through the images I took today for the cover edition. I am a bundle of nerves and excitement as I think about my work being presented on the magazine cover.

I feel so blessed to have this opportunity, being able to present my work on the cover of the magazine is beyond what I dreamed was possible, but it's so much more than that. These brilliant images are invaluable to me. I imagine I am capturing 'time' in the most perfect moments; a fraction of a second that passes so quickly in people's lives. It brings me such a sense of peace and satisfaction knowing these images will be present for many, many more generations to come.

The images flash before me as I determine the best ones for the cover submission; the beautiful day with the golden sun resting brightly over the park as it illuminates the lake, children running with colourful kites in tow, and parents sitting on rugs with delightful picnics laid out. Love, life and laughter emanates from each photo as the images light up my computer screen and bring a genuine smile to my face. "Photography takes me to such a special place; a peaceful, tranquil place. This job and this opportunity – living here in this unique coastal town with the most incredible people is exactly what I need and where I want to be right now." I smile softly in retrospect of my journey here.

"I missed so much of my life and endless opportunities as I completely lost myself, stuck in my own endless loop. A black hole so strong that nothing could escape it," I consider. *"You're not lost beautiful, your just on a detour. One that will lead you exactly to where you need to be. Be patient baby girl."* Flynn reminds me as I reflect on his advice and traverse through to the present.

"Flynn, you were right." I smile happily to myself as I hit send to the editor on my final submission for the cover.

Maverick

I make my way up to the stage; the lights blind me for an instant as I place myself on the stool and perch with my guitar. I adjust the strings, tuning my acoustic as I sit quietly, ready to play.

Tonight, I want to sing for her, my whole existence at the moment is because of her. I feel lighter than I have been in years. It feels as if my self-destruct, worthless button has been turned off, if only for a short while – but it feels fucking incredible to be free of the hate and relentless anger battering me and just embrace each day. One single day at a time.

The universe is complete straight up asshole as I've finally found a reason to live again, I can finally breathe again and it's absolutely because of her, but it's too late. I know the angel of death is watching over my shoulder and waiting for me, although I've come too far in this now to tell her the truth. It's going to break her completely and fuck that, I do not want her to shed a single tear because of me.

She is my entire fucking world right now and I would walk through the entire depths of hell if nothing else but just to see her smile.

She has experienced pain in its purest form, been hurt beyond imagination and yet found the strength to carry on and shown me what it is to love again, what it is to change the demons in your past and turn them into something beautiful, something so passionate and real. Isabelle lives her life each day with the motto that 'the next day will always be better than yesterday,' as she looks at the world in admiration and wonder. She is the strongest woman I know as she picks herself back up and dusts herself off – every single time the world takes her down.

I am completely lost in her and entirely in love with her.

I know she's stolen my heart completely, I would happily rip it from my chest and give it to her gladly; she owns my entire world and has me on my knees. This scares me more than anything I've ever experienced. I'm fucking scared out of mind how to tell her. "How do you tell someone you love them with everything you are, but then add the fucked-up caveat – you cannot stay?" It fucking hurts like hell even thinking about it.

Each day it weighs on me heavily and I'm leaning towards calling Arizona and letting her in, letting her help me. Arizona has always said this is not the end of the line for me, maybe now my anger has subsided a little more and I'm thinking a little more rationally, I could at least hear her out and the options she believes I should consider.

There is so much I need to tell Isabelle and she's never going to understand, it's far too late. "How do I tell someone I love them when it's too late?" My mind races with these thoughts as I search for her in the rising crowd.

I finally spot her sitting with Walter tonight in a booth a few rows back from the stage. I'm so honoured that Walters' here and he's come to see me, this makes me wholeheartedly smile as I hope I make him proud tonight.

Isabelle beams up at me. Holy fucking hell, she slams the breath right out of me every time she looks at me with her bright blue eyes and beautiful smile. Her blonde wavy hair moves as she shakes her head with laughter at something Walter has said. She's wearing her favourite blue ripped denim jeans and a turquoise tank top with an array of beads hanging around her neck. She looks stunning. There is no other woman who comes close to comparing with her. I'm utterly disgusted the way I treated women before I met her, "Another thing I will never tell her." I sigh, as she meets my gaze and smiles back, waving happily.

I strum my guitar and the crowd cheers as I begin the first lines to Ron Pope – A Drop in The Ocean. As I work through the melody; Every. Single. Thought. Is. About. Her.

She is my *own* heaven.

As the song draws to a close and I sing the final chorus, I glance up from my guitar and spot them before Isabelle or Walter do.

A deep pain resonates in my chest as I let myself be happy for this moment in time. Although it was inevitable, the moments of happiness I spent with Isabelle is worth all the anguish that is to come. My only regret is the pain I'm going to cause her now as I promised myself and her – that I would never intentionally hurt her. If I could shield her, keep her safe and protect her always – I would burn down the entire fucking universe if that's what it took. This time though – it is me burning. I am the one that's catching fire as my past catches up with me.

The local sheriff is standing in the doorway of the venue accompanied by Detective Ryland.

I sigh and nod at Detective Ryland, acknowledging his presence, not wanting to cause a major scene as I know there is only one outcome here. It is real and I have no where left to run from this. I silently pray that Isabelle doesn't cry as I place my guitar gently back in the case and step off the stage, my combat boots heavier with each step as I make my way over to her.

Isabelle jumps up and swings her arms around me. "That was incredibly beautiful as always Mav!" She beams as she kisses my cheek. I hug her closely, inhaling her scent as I whisper in her ear, "Isabelle, I have to go now, but I promise you I will be back. I *will* come back for you."

I slowly peel her arms from around my neck and look her in the eyes. "I promise you Isabelle." Her eyes widen in confusion.

"Where are you going Mav?" she probes.

"What actually is the answer to that?" I think to myself, do I even know where I am heading?

"Mav?" she repeats, as she squeezes my hand and gazes up at me with sadness and confusion. Detective Ryland moves closer and places his hand on my shoulder as I lean in and kiss Isabelle's cheek.

"I'm so very sorry songbird," I whisper in her ear. "I'm sorry." Is all I can manage to say as the sheriff places my wrists in handcuffs and begins to read me my rights.

Walter steps forward. "Maverick son, what happened?" he urges. I stare at the ground ashamed. My past has caught up with me and I've hurt the two people who opened their lives and hearts to me. Isabelle's eyes sparkle with unshed tears.

"No, wait!" she urges the sheriff. "This is a mistake," she whispers. "Maverick tell them, please," she pleads.

Isabelle grabs my waist and peers up at me, "Please Mav, tell me what's going on?" Detective Ryland grabs her shoulder gently and tells her to calm down. He motions for her to step aside and calmly explains she will be detained if she continues to hinder my arrest, quietly explaining they do have a warrant.

I feel like I'm drowning at this point, lost underneath the waves in the depths of the darkest ocean. There are not enough words or time to take back what I have done and the pain on Isabelle's face is cutting through me like a jagged knife.

"I'm so sorry Walter, take care of Isabelle please," I beg as I turn to face him, hands secured behind my back. He nods solemnly in return but says nothing. I never meant to hurt him or anyone.

"I fuck everything up, like a wildfire that burns everything in its path," I think to myself as my head starts pounding. "I feel like I am on fire, the cinders etched throughout my bones with the flames burning deep into my chest and exploding in my head."

I slowly turn to face Isabelle. "Isabelle, I can explain and I *will* songbird," I plead honestly with her.

She lets me go and slowly moves her head up to face me as she wraps her arms protectively around herself. "Maverick. You told me you would never hurt me?" she whispers.

"You lied," she murmurs simply as a tear rolls down her face.

At that very moment my heart and mind shatters into a thousand pieces, my head is pounding like the beat of a drum and I can't take a single breath. "I can't breathe," I whisper as my body doubles over in pain. I feel Detective Ryland loosen his hold on me as I crash to my knees. Hands gently guide me down onto the hard timber floor as I'm rolled onto my side. I convulse with absolute pain as the pitch blackness engulfs me until there is nothing. Nothing at all.

Isabelle

I lie in the grass on the back lawn and stare at the sky for hours;
I haven't taken a single picture since he left.
I don't do anything anymore.
I am empty.
I am lost.
I give up.

Isabelle

"Isabelle?" Madison questions from the back patio sliding door of my parent's holiday house.

I don't answer. "What's the point? Everybody has tried to talk to me, tried to make me feel better. I don't care, I have nothing more to give," I think to myself, resigned.

The last few months are a blank page. I can't remember a single moment, a single day since he was taken away. Not a single memory. Well not a happy one anyway. I've heard your brain attempts to protect you from trauma, but I believe this must be intricately linked with your heart as mine is irrevocably broken. Shattered into a million pieces and lost within the sirocco winds – no single piece will ever find its way back to each other again.

The pain I feel is overwhelming, the emptiness tears at me every day and my heart needs time. "Time for what?" I ponder. My experiences and emotional wounds feel as deep as the Mariana trench and I don't believe 'time' will ever be enough to heal these scars.

"I remember in high school learning about Earths deepest places, one of them hidden in the Pacific Ocean. It is said, humans cannot withstand the intense pressure of the trench itself; the sheer force will collapse any space in your body filled with air and that – is certainly how I feel right now," I think sadly. "I'm being continuously squeezed and the pressure is sucking the life out of me."

"She's down there." I hear Madison tell someone.

I really hope it's not another someone trying to make me 'feel' better. The attempts at understanding and 'you will be okay' advice has been endless. I know people want to help and I truly appreciate they care, but it's not helping. At all.

I despise him and I loathe myself. "I am angry with the entire universe," now I actually think about it. Life shouldn't be this hard and nothing anyone wants to talk about will make that better.

"Hi beautiful." A deep rich familiar voice reaches my ears. Someone is standing directly over me as a shadow crosses my body. I open my eyes and squint as I sit up slowly and turn. I know that voice but cannot place it yet as the sun is blocking my view. I use my hands in an attempt to shield my eyes from the blinding sun and focus harder. He's tall, muscular, tattooed and very tanned I surmise as my brain attempts to make sense of this. I squint in silence attempting to focus, trying to bring his face into view.

"I won't take it personally Isabelle, most girls *are* stunned into silence when they see me," he laughs. "I take their breath away," he whispers as he bends down and kisses me on the cheek gently.

"Flynn!" I jump up with recognition and hug him so tightly. I think he can't breathe from my iron grip as he chuckles. "What are you doing here?" I exclaim as his strong arms embrace me.

"I told you sunshine, I will find you, and I found you." He smiles as he kisses my cheek again and brings me back in for a fierce hug, then out again to inspect me with a generous smile.

He looks me in the eyes and continues, "So… I hear we have some catching up to do?" Flynn raises his eyebrow at me in concern. "Nope, nothing much to talk about." I sigh and stare at the ground. I don't want to talk about him anymore, it rips at what is left of my black, cold heart. I know Flynn would be ashamed of me… if only he knew what has happened since I left the island.

The strong, determined girl he knew when I left the island is now a shell of a person. She has no dreams, no aspiration and no understanding of life. "Life is a cutthroat bitch," I surmise, "and I give up." I think dejectedly.

"Trust is a powerful emotion and I let my guard down (again) and Maverick stole my happiness in the blink of an eye."

Isabelle

"So, you have a secret life full of 'Super-Incredibly-Hot-Guy-Friends' and don't think to tell another soul?" Madison laughs as she emphasises each word and attempts to curl my damaged hair.

I laugh. "No Madison, Flynn is just a friend from the island and if I had a black book of hot friends you know that Skylar would have stolen the book already," I reply with a sad attempt at a smile.

"You know what Isabelle, that's the first time you've laughed in over a month," Madison replies with a smile and tears in her eyes.

"Don't be sad Madison please, I'm okay, I promise. I wish everyone would stop fussing," I reply as I turn to face her.

"What? So everyone would leave you here to fade away like you wish for? I don't think so," she states harshly.

"I don't want to disappear Madison, I just don't know how to be me right now. I guess I just don't know how to move forward yet?" I stutter anxiously. This is the longest conversation I've had in six weeks and I'm feeling drained after a few sentences.

"Look Flynn is a friend; he's seen me at my worst and been there when times were really tough for me. I owe it to him to, to... I don't know, try and be a normal human for a few days while he's here," I reply. "I will try really hard tonight to be happy and enjoy the night out." I state genuinely. "Please just give me time and no more talking about Mav... for tonight?" I whisper.

Madison softens, her harsh glare replaced with a look of sorrow as I continue, "I am truly sorry Madison, I don't mean to hurt everyone around me and be such a burden." I pause and let out a breath as Madison sits down on the bed deflated.

"I know you put your life on hold for me, to be here and support me, and I am eternally grateful. Although I don't have the words right now for you Madison, someday I will find a way to truly repay your kindness. You shouldn't worry about me, I've got this, I promise." I whisper. "Don't waste your time here with me Madison," I plead.

"You have Cruize and a whole exciting adventure waiting ahead for you." I smile.

"That's not fair Isabelle, I want to be here for you and you push me away. You push everyone away Isabelle when it gets hard," Madison protests. Her words sending a jolt of pain through me that radiates with truth deep down into my spine. "I know you want to be here for me Madison, but you can't put your life on hold for me. I'm fine. I swear it, please believe me," I plead, hoping she accepts my false bravado and ends this difficult conversation.

I'm not ready to deal with my emotions and this conversation is taking me to the edge. The urge to flee again is incredibly powerful as my internal battle rages. I don't know how to move forward, I don't know how to find me again and I am struggling to pick up the broken pieces whilst completely lost in a jungle of despair. Again.

Madison hasn't left my side in six weeks, lost her job and almost Cruize due to my stubborn and selfish, gloomy state I wallow in. I can't even begin to comprehend how to drag myself out of the darkness this time, it has a hold so fierce on me – but my shadows have no right to darken everyone around me.

"Flynn is a sign," I tell her positively. "A sign that things are looking up." I smile. "Things *will* be better Madison, I promise. Please don't be sad," I whisper as I pull her in for a deep embrace. We wrap our arms tightly around each other as the tense atmosphere between us fades away.

Flynn interrupts our moment with a light tap on the door, "Ladies are we ready to drink, laugh and love?" he yells from behind the door.

"God Skylar would love to show him a good time," Madison whispers mischievously and laughs at her own comment as she kisses me on the cheek. "I really can't believe you never told us about him Isabelle, he's so wonderful. He's kind, funny, intelligent and most importantly a beautiful soul – he truly cares about you Isabelle," she states honestly.

She's right, he's all of those things but he's also my friend, my confidant, my saviour and guiding angel. There is nothing I want to do to jeopardise the friendship and incredible bond I've found with Flynn.

People walk into your life for a reason, and I honestly believe Flynn walked into mine on that tiny island, (or as fate would have it, I actually crashed right into him baggage and all) when I needed him the most, and he has irreversibly left tiny imprints on my heart.

I think of Flynn and our relationship as an unbreakable bond between two souls, no matter the distance that separates us, we are destined to walk our journey together, wherever it may take us – through the good times and the bad.

"I know," I reply. "Let's go before I change my mind." I laugh as I open the bathroom door and give Flynn a huge smile and a bear hug whilst he laughs softly, showing off his attractive dimples as he rubs his hand through his wild blonde hair.

I look up at him and genuinely appreciate that he is actually here with me, no longer hidden within my jumbled mind, giving me a gentle push, providing whispers of encouragement in my ear... as vivid memories flash before me. Flynn stands strong beside me, like a pillar of strength, physically here with me in this moment. He found me – as promised on the island jetty, and remarkably, he found me when I needed him the most.

He winks at Madison, and I know with that one look entirely what he is saying to her: "I've got this." Although I don't think he truly understands just how far I've fallen since I left the island, but I let him have this moment, and I embrace him again, tighter than before, just for a while longer before the dam completely collapses.

We are all going to the local bar for dinner and a few drinks. I staged a futile protest for about four hours prior as I know the bar will only bring back a flood of painful memories... every single reminder of him. But everyone insisted it's the best venue close by and the whole crew is looking forward to a night out, followed by the stumble home under the stars – with no designated drivers tonight. I reluctantly agreed to this adventure eventually, knowing in my mind that I wanted to prove to Flynn that I am strong and I haven't fallen helplessly apart since I left the island. "A complete lie," I think to myself, but how hard can it be to put on a brave face for one night.

We arrive at the bar around eight p.m. and I am terrified. Literally frozen with fear even looking at the front door.

His music and his soul took me to a magical place; he was my entire world, my breath of fresh air and the ocean breeze across my body on a hot summers' day. He brought light into my life and gifted me reasons to move forward, trust again and open my heart back up. I felt like I could finally breathe again. Now as

I stand here, incapable of taking another step through those doors – I cannot even fathom being in this place where we created these memories together.

It hurts and the anger bubbles away as I wonder where he is right now. "Is he okay? Why was he arrested? And why did he keep such a secret from me?" I think about these questions uncertain and confused. My mind continues to haunt me with these unknowns, as I reflect on how I also held so much back from him out of fear, although I was not even close to understanding that perhaps – his secrets were considerably worse than mine. Our relationship in retrospect therefore lacked two very significant features – communication and trust. I know deep inside I was not completely open with him, my memories and experiences are so very painful and I lack the skills to communicate my feelings. "Perhaps that's why he was not honest with me?" I wonder. These questions plague my mind that I may never know the answer to, nor how to deal with.

Unnervingly, I don't even know what he was charged with, all I knew is that he lied to me. An act of omission of something this important is akin to lying. I promised myself I would never be with a liar ever again. I would never lower my guard, never let anyone through my defences and never let someone in that could possibly hurt me. "That didn't work out so well," I think sadly.

Maverick slowly and patiently broke down my walls and I have no one else to blame but myself – I let him in. I realise now I loved him and a piece of my heart and soul is missing. He was my anchor through the stormy nights, he was my lighthouse when I was couldn't find my way, and he was my mast when I needed to stand tall and be brave.

He was my everything.

I never told Maverick any of that, and if I regret anything at all, it is that I never mustered the courage to tell him how I truly felt. Beyond all of the anger and confusion I feel now, if I'm being completely honest with myself, I know that even through these addled thoughts and bleary eyes – I still love him. I miss him achingly every single day and I have no idea how to take my heart back, piece it back together and return it to where it belongs. I fear it will never be reassembled to what it once was, knowing my heart completely belongs to him now. I gave it to him willingly, tiny piece by piece... a long time ago.

"Hey princess, are we going in or hanging out here tonight?" Flynn interrupts my train wreck of thoughts as he asks with a concerned look. His eyebrow raised as I stand motionless at the entrance to the bar.

Flynn gently pulls me in for a hug. He wraps his warm body and strong arms around me before I can respond. "I'm here now Isabelle. I'm here beautiful," he whispers in my ear. I snap out of my trance and smile that Flynn is *actually* here with me. The voice that has supported me in my head every step of the way since I left island... is finally here. I feel content with Flynn here beside me, and I think maybe, just maybe – the universe is not a complete asshole today.

"Sorry Flynn, I was in another place. Yes, let's go." I smile, plastering it on my face, knowing he can see right through me like cellophane.

We enter the bar together as everyone has gone ahead of us. I scan the room immediately, praying silently I don't see him (or so I tell myself that in encouragement). "It's highly unlikely," I consider, although I am wildly unprepared for it. I have no idea what I would do if I see him again.

I feel like I'm going to have an anxiety attack at the very thought of even laying my eyes on him. My heart constricts and my chest feels tighter with every breath. "God I miss him with everything I am," I think silently.

"Just breathe baby girl, everything will be okay. I promise you," Flynn whispers quietly in my ear. It is as if Flynn can feel my tension, and understand my emotions as he gently grabs my hand in the safety of his own. Flynn gives me an encouraging nod and we make our way over to the bar.

"I'm buying!" states Cruize enthusiastically as he saunters over to meet us at the bar with Madison and Skylar happily in tow.

"What's your poison love?" Flynn asks as he peers down and looks me in the eyes.

"Anything strong," I reply quietly, not really paying attention with my thoughts still locked on Maverick. "I will find a booth for us to sit in." I smile and walk away slowly towards an empty booth, enough to seat five of us.

I scoot over within the bench seat, moving to sit closest to the window, a safety net of sorts that both surrounds me with people I know and trust, yet lets me stare out the window when I can no longer hold a conversation, unable to contribute where socially appropriate.

I scan the bar again whilst I sit alone waiting for the group to return when Luna approaches and slides into the booth next to me. "Hey lovely, how are you?" she asks.

"Good thanks and you?" I reply as standard.

"We've missed you, you know? I haven't seen you in a long time, is everything okay?" she enquires. "Perhaps she's already heard the latest gossip?" I seethe to myself.

Prying me for information is not going to work. I know I'm being dramatic as Luna is certainly not the type to pry and genuinely does care, but with walls this high, she's basically scaling the Great Pyramid of Giza right now as my negative thoughts snake through my mind.

"Fine thanks Luna, just busy you know." I smile, hoping the questions (attempted interrogation in my brain) trail off.

I respect Luna but I don't have any answers right now. Not for her and certainly not for me. "Okay, well if you need anything, just let me know sweetie," she replies as she scoots out of the booth and walks back to her spot behind the bar.

Everyone returns from the bar full of energy and laughter as they slide into the booth around me. I smile and nod and pretend to pay attention, but my mind is still warped elsewhere, even with Flynn here.

Flynn is a natural presence amongst the group, it is like he's been a part of the crew forever. He fits in well and even manages to tactfully deflect Skylar's obvious flirting which makes me irrationally happy, but also frustrated at the same time. I can't even have a friend that's not off limits to her. "Maybe she just hasn't found her person yet?" I contemplate, but still, her advances are not called for. Although Flynn seems to take it all in his stride, like it's the most normal thing is the world to have complete strangers fawning over you. I know he's not short of a lady friend, and most women in the bar have already stopped to shamelessly inspect the new addition in town, but I feel a somewhat unreasonable protectiveness of him regardless of who it is that approaches him.

My mindless trail of negative thoughts are interrupted abruptly – when I see him enter.

"Maverick." I breathe quietly.

I'm stuck at the back of the booth, trapped near the window. As I cannot immediately flee the situation I begin to feel an entire new level of alarm, my internal panic stations reaching defcon one in the blink of an eye. I try unsuccessfully to even out my breathing as the anxiety quickly takes a strong and successful hold. "Just breathe Isabelle, that's all you need to do." I chant this silently to myself and hold back unshed tears.

My palms are sweating and I am rubbing my hands together so tightly they change colour. If I could also see my reflection in a mirror, I am confident I would be deathly pale as I feel the life force rush out of me.

I glance up slowly, watching him walk over to the bar and pull out a stool as he sits in solitude. "He looks different," I observe silently, attempting unsuccessfully to avoid him and all thoughts of him. He seems much skinnier and his hair is tousled; whilst minor details, Maverick always prided himself on his physical health and well-being. "He is not holding himself like he normally does with a 'fuck-you-world' attitude and the confidence of a demigod."

Something is very wrong.

"Are you okay princess?" Flynn whispers in my ear.

"No, I need some air," I whisper back.

"Okay let's go outside for a minute," he replies and ushers Skylar out of the booth beside him. Flynn informs everyone we are just getting some air for a moment as he grabs his coat.

No one pays attention except for Skylar who huffs in disapproval of Flynn's momentary absence. Skylar shuffles back into the booth once Flynn and I have scooted out of our seats. They are all engrossed, completely wrapped up in the latest local gossip, not noticing his presence like I do.

They didn't notice at all.

He's like a wildfire that entered the bar, an unplanned inferno that I was unprepared for. Mavericks fire ingrains itself in every bone within my body, once again taking siege upon my heart and claiming my soul. Every sense within me sparks to life, although I am entirely lost as to what my external response will be. I don't know how to react – I want to go to him, support him, wrap my arms around him and know that he is unharmed. But regardless of what I *want* to do, my feelings of anger and distrust keep me at bay whilst my tears threaten to rush out of me; a complete chaos of emotions.

I stand to grab my winter coat and bag. I reach up beside the booth to the rustic coat hooks, collecting my belongings as I curiously peer over to Maverick again whilst he sits facing the bar. Flynn kindly helps shuffle my coat on, although my focus is elsewhere as he gently wraps the coat around my shoulders. I can see Mavericks side profile more clearly now and he looks drawn and tired; his dark hair is haphazardly over his face, his eyes black as the darkest night. He looks as lawless as the ocean storms and lost within the most turbulent seas. He appears painfully thin in his face, and his eyes sunken like he hasn't slept in days. He twirls his lip ring around slowly whilst staring into nothingness.

My heart lurches towards him and I know it shouldn't, but there is nothing I can do to control these emotions and what I feel for him, buried underneath all of my anger and hurt.

I can see his intricate and captivating tattoos snaking up his arm and reappearing at his neck. Dark and detailed ink peeks out from underneath his crisp, white collared shirt and extends all the way from his neck back down to his wrist.

"It is a hell of a lot more scripture and detail than I've noticed before. The black ink streams towards his hand, even from afar it looks dangerous and menacing... just like him," I consider. I stand motionless, wondering if it could even be written in a dead language, or scribed in Egyptian hieroglyphics as I continue my silent observations from a distance. My curious mind ticks into overdrive; wondering what the ink represents and how it impacts him.

I'm hypnotically drawn to him again like a bee finds pollen. "His tattoos add another aura of mystery and complicated layer to him. It is so incredibly attractive, although I should not be attracted to him – at all." I scold myself. "He is the one who caused this pain and I know I cannot be with him," I think dejectedly. "Forgiveness seems to be keeping me prisoner... bound within the tightest chains. I cannot forgive him. Can I? I'm so angry and hurt, I'm confused and sad – my brain is a broken kaleidoscope of emotions right now," I think troublingly, without any real answers.

"Why is everything so hard?" I sigh as Flynn and I step outside into the cold, winter night air and start walking along the gravel pathway. I move ever so slowly, entirely lost within my own thoughts. I shove my hands deep in my pockets for warmth and a sense of security, my boots heavy with every step I take further away from Maverick.

Flynn doesn't speak a single word as we walk. He is as patient as always with his hand gently on my back, guiding me along the gravel pathway under the light of the stars.

We make our way through the main street and down into the park overlooking the lake. It's dimly lit at this time of night, but I can see the lake shimmering ahead with the moonlight leading the way, knowing, that's where I need to be right now.

I walk over to the lush grass and untie my laces, slipping my boots off as we continue down the embankment. My bare feet embrace the earth until we reach a familiar, timber park bench, perfectly located closest to the lake. Flynn sits and I proceed to lie down on the bench seat with my head comfortably across his lap. I close my eyes as he runs his hands gently through my hair.

Everything is uncomplicated and effortless with Flynn. I always feel protected and safe within his orbit, yet a tear escapes my eye, falling silently down my face and onto his lap as soon as he asks.

"Was that him?"

"Who?" I reply quietly.

"Maverick?" he questions. I take a deep breath and hold it, breathless as I hear his name escape Flynn's lips.

"Yes." I exhale. "How did you know?" I whisper ever so quietly.

"Isabelle." Flynn smiles. "Your friends care deeply for you, and they filled me in when I arrived. No secrets here, only you baby girl," he replies quietly. Flynn continues stroking my hair as he continues, "Look princess, I know I haven't been here for you, and I know you've come a long way since the island life, but you should give him a chance... and talk to him?" he requests.

"What. Why?" I reply angrily as I sit up and face him. "Flynn, he hurt me. He lied. Did you know he was arrested?" I shoot back defensively and look him in the eyes – mine filled with tears, his brimming with sadness.

"I know," he replies slowly as he takes my hand in his and cups my cheek with his other hand. "Yet let me ask you something beautiful – did you open up to him and tell him how you felt? Everything you went through?" he asks as he grabs both my hands within his. Flynn's words strike like arrows, hitting their target without mercy as he already knows the answers to each of those questions.

"Isabelle, you can't expect someone to tell you their dreams, their hopes, their fears and their mistakes – if you're not willing to do the same," he continues. "Belle," Flynn sighs with a smile and he gazes at me with his boundless blue eyes. "You're the most stubborn, determined, driven, passionate and strongest person I have ever met, but there are times when you don't need to always be strong, and there are also times when you need to back down," he explains. Flynn places a gentle kiss on my cheek as tears stream down my face.

"Flynn, I don't understand?" I whisper. "Why are you taking his side? You've never met him, and you have no idea of the things he has done," I fume.

"Baby girl. I'm telling you this – for you. He's made mistakes, but you will never know what the future holds if you don't talk to him. You should hear this from him Belle, but apparently you refuse to talk to him, or about him, so I'm telling you." He sighs and looks up at the stars illuminating the night sky for a few moments. I get the impression he's considering whether or not to continue talking. I wait patiently, holding my breath until I finally muster the courage and ask.

"What is it Flynn?"

"If I was less like me." He laughs. "Or any other man on the entire planet," he continues. "I wouldn't tell you this, but your happiness means more to me than anything else, so I need you to *hear* me Isabelle," he urges. "Please listen before you react," he finishes. I absorb his powerful words and nod slowly, fully understanding that this is something Flynn truly wants me to know, so I stay silent and wait for him.

"He was released more than two weeks ago Belle. He was found completely not guilty, in fact, they had accused him of crimes that were impossible for him to have committed based on his whereabouts at the time. All the charges against him were dropped. I'm not saying he is a saint Isabelle, but he did not commit these crimes," Flynn explains as he peers across at me.

"What do you mean charges? What was he accused of?" I ask quietly, my heart beating faster.

The answers I need, but not sure I want, or are ready for – are within reach. But I'm afraid, I'm emotionally exhausted and not sure I can carry the burden this cargo holds. The mental exhaustion weighs on me each and every day as I muddle through this pain and try to understand what went wrong.

"How did I let my guard down again, and how did I let myself get so hurt – how did he break through my fortress walls I tirelessly built?" I think to myself over and over.

"You don't even know the charges Isabelle?" Flynn interrupts my internal battle, surprised by my question. "I never wanted to know. I was too scared to ask the night they arrived with a warrant for his arrest, stealing him away from me." I remember the moment unhappily. I thought knowing would break me irreversibly. So, I never asked.

"No Flynn, I never asked why they took him away," I whisper as I stare down at our hands now intertwined.

Flynn sighs and waits another moment. "Isabelle, he was charged with aggravated assault and theft at the time he was arrested. He was overdue in court and failed to appear some thousands of miles away, hence why he was arrested at the bar – for failing to appear upon a court summons. You should ask him the rest Belle." He smiles and wipes the tears away from my eyes.

"Flynn, I can't," I stammer in between tears.

"Isabelle, you will spend the rest of your life regretting it if you don't. You need to know. If nothing else, it will give you closure. Talk to him Isabelle, the good, the bad, it doesn't matter – your soul won't rest until you have made peace with this. You love him Isabelle, I can see this clear as a full moon, regardless of the darkest clouds on a pitch-black night, even if you won't acknowledge it." Flynn smiles with his dimples on full display as he raises his eyebrow, knowing his words ring true.

"It's time beautiful; pick your heart back up and return it to where it belongs." He smiles as he kisses me on the cheek gently.

Flynn pulls me closer, bringing me into his warm arms like a blanket of comfort and security. I rest my head on his chest and feel his arms wrapped safely around me – although this entirely feels like a 'goodbye'.

Isabelle

"Flynn?" I whisper in his ear quietly.
It's six a.m. and I can't sleep...
Flynn's words weigh heavily on my mind. Confusion and guilt burrow deep into the recesses of my mind; alike concrete pillars being drilled into solid earth, over and over again throughout the night.

He's right in so many ways as I reflect on what Flynn said earlier, it resounds through my mind as the dawn approaches.

"Yet let me ask you something beautiful – did you open up to him and tell him how you felt? Everything you went through?... Isabelle, you can't expect someone to tell you their dreams, their hopes, their fears and their mistakes – if you're not willing to do the same."

It's absolutely true and Flynn always knows what to say. I have not been fair at all, and far too hasty to judge when I have my own personal demons to accept, none of which I have ever shared with Maverick. Flynn was right, my soul aches to be with Maverick, and I know I won't rest until I make peace with this – regardless of the outcome.

"I know Maverick has stolen my heart for an eternity, and it belongs to him now," I acknowledge. A huge smile crosses my face as the butterflies awaken in my stomach. I willingly handed my heart over to him, piece by piece until he captured it entirely. I know I love him with everything I am. I have fallen for him endlessly... but I have no idea how to tell him *any* of this.

"I need to talk to Maverick," I decide. There is a life force pulling me towards him. I feel butterflies in my stomach when I think of him, my heart beats faster when I see him, my mind races with intrigue when he speaks, and my emotions go haywire when he sings. I'm angry and hurt, but Flynn is right, I need to make peace with what has happened or I will live in agony for the rest of my life not knowing… without Maverick.

"Destiny," I think to myself. "Flynn has always guided me towards the right path." I smile as I kiss him gently on the cheek while he sleeps and I leave a note as I gratefully take his advice.

Flynn,

Following destiny,

Isabelle xx

It's so cold outside, the winter chill reaching my bones as the crisp air whips around my face. I walk swiftly and drag my winter jacket higher up to protect my ears from the wind as I tentatively approach the magnificent warehouse. It is well illuminated, highlighting where Maverick lives in the early hours of the morning with the sunrise breaking its way through the ominous clouds in the background.

I take a brisk pace and arrive a little less confident with each step of my magenta boots, wondering what I'm actually doing here. I stand motionless at the bottom of the warehouse steps, reminiscing about the first time he marched up them with his heavy black combat boots. My mind melts at the memory of his thoughtfulness and my body reacting to everything that is Maverick.

I take a deep breath, not knowing what to expect and walk up the steps quietly. "He's probably asleep, this is stupid," I think as I tap lightly on the door.

"No answer." I sigh after a few minutes of waiting.

My moment of courage has all but evaporated when I hear movement inside the warehouse. I tap again lightly on the door and try the handle. It's unlocked, so I push the door ever so slightly and it creaks open loudly into the warehouse.

I peer around the huge industrial door and spot Maverick perched on a stool at the kitchen island bench. "Isabelle?" he whispers in astonishment as his eyes widen at the sight of me.

"Maverick," I stutter, feeling entirely lost for words in this moment, as I stand at his mercy at his door. Everything else disappears before me except him. His dark eyes focus solely on me. Maverick twirls his lip ring within his fingers, displaying his usual trait, whilst his spoon dangles precariously over his porridge as he stares intensely at me.

He's only wearing a pair of black tracksuit pants and I'm finding it hard to concentrate on anything other than his body at this point. "What are you doing here?" he asks as he moves off the stool towards me.

I stand motionless, grasping the door like a life raft for support. "I wanted to talk," I state, my voice shaky. I'm not sure whether he's happy or shocked I'm here. I'm petrified, although fighting every urge in my body not to flee right now.

"Maverick, we need to organise the bathroom stuff today." A voice interrupts.

A female voice echoes from further down the hallway. She appears a moment later at the hallway entrance. "Maverick, did you hear me?" she asks as she stops abruptly, realising I'm standing in the doorway. Her eyes meet mine, filled with surprise.

She's incredibly beautiful, tall with long dark hair, wrapped in only a towel and drying her hair with another. "She could be a supermodel," I surmise silently. Her eyes are dark and defined, her legs are long and slender and her face is chiselled like a work of art. She is radiant.

"God, there is no way I can compete with her." I cringe in my head. I've been gone almost two months and he's found her. "I thought I was something to him," I think painfully.

Once again, stupid naive me believed that we shared something unique. Something so special, no one else could possibly understand. Flynn patiently attempted to mend the pieces of my heart back together and gave me the strength to try again – all of which shattered in this instant.

"Sorry Maverick. I'm so sorry I interrupted. I've got to go," I splutter as I turn and race out the door.

"Isabelle, wait. It's not what you think," he yells after me as I reach the bottom steps and sprint along the pavement. I hear Maverick thump down the warehouse steps two at a time behind me.

"Isabelle. Stop," he urges.

"Please," he sighs defeated.

Tears stream down my face as I slow my pace and eventually come to a complete stop. I feel humiliated.

I love him entirely and yet he has a beautiful girl in his shower. "God. I'm so fucking ridiculous," I think to myself, wondering why I halted my escape after hearing his voice.

"Isabelle." He breathes as I slowly turn and he stalks towards me down the road. Maverick grabs my face with both his hands and rest his forehead on mine. He's still only wearing a dark pair of tracksuit pants with no shirt and no shoes. His body is causing a conflicting riot in my brain.

"Your all I want. Believe me when I say that," he breathes. "There's so much you don't know songbird." He looks down into my eyes. "And I don't know how to tell you." He finishes.

Maverick pulls me closer and grabs my waist tightly. He presses his lips to mine as he advances further towards me, and pulls me dangerously closer, our bodies connecting as he lights a fire of hope within me at the same time. He runs his hand softly down my face and wipes away my tears gently as he holds me close and we stand motionless together.

Maverick kisses my face, smells my hair and breathes me in. I don't understand as he slowly pulls away and whispers in my ear, "We can't be Isabelle …. and it breaks my heart – please know that. I'm so very sorry songbird, but know that I will always be yours. Always and forever in my heart." He finishes as he kisses my forehead softly and slowly releases me from our embrace.

Maverick reluctantly releases me as he turns to walk away without another word, and my heart silently shatters into a thousand pieces with every step he takes away from me. I fall to my knees and sit on the road sobbing. I don't entirely understand what just transpired, although what I do know – is that – was a 'goodbye.'

Isabelle

I'm moving home with my parents. I've applied for a job on a cruise ship. "What better place to live out my misery," I think to myself, "than the middle of the ocean." I laugh.

"What a mess I've made of things." Madison and Skylar are helping me pack, I've accumulated quite a lot of stuff since living here and I need to prepare my portfolio for my interview, with a pending departure, if successful, in eight weeks.

I've applied for one of the highly sought-after positions – the cruise ships' professional photographer. This includes prepping images from travels abroad to showcase on the website and use in targeted marketing campaigns. In addition, the job requires the professional photographer to be present on the ship from port to port, capturing guest images – to be purchased for a highly inflated price.

Flynn left shortly after Mavericks 'goodbye' and my subsequent meltdown; he's always been a free spirit, guided by his own intuition. Flynn told me he loved me, and wants to spend the rest of his life making me happy, but he knows my heart entirely belongs to someone else.

With those complicated emotions left lingering in the air – Flynn travelled home shortly after. I was too heartbroken to even acknowledge his presence, so I'm surprised he even talks to me at all. Flynn is perfect, but he's not my perfect, and I only wish him all the best life has to offer. I know we will meet again, and hopefully I can be the person I want to be when we do.

I have one last photo shoot to add to my portfolio before I leave this unique coastal town. I turned the editor down time and time again, but with the insistence that I take the final shoot to increase my portfolio, and a generous amount of money on offer, I reluctantly agreed.

The photo shoot appointment was two weeks ago, but the editor allowed me to delay so I could organise moving. I don't understand the importance of this particular shoot but the client was accommodating – so I eventually I agreed. The more I can improve my portfolio, the more opportunities I will have, although once again, photography is no longer a passionate affair for me. Photography was about encapsulating life's specials moments, brief nanoseconds in time, captured perfectly to reflect; joy, happiness, sadness, people, experiences, life and passion. I believe you need to feel that spark within yourself to truly capture those moments for others. However, my spark is broken, my flame extinguished as I wander in the dark. My emptiness is like a black cloud, it hovers precariously above me with every heavy step I take – feeling as though my boots are made of lead. Taking even a single photograph, and pouring my heart into an image, is almost impossible now.

I lost my soul and passion when Maverick said goodbye, which makes photography an emotionless task now, but I'm resigned to the fact – I cannot give up. I will not give up. As Flynn would say, *"straighten your crown princess and be brave. Move forward one day at a time, no matter how painful that day will be – you are stronger than you think."*

Madison, Skylar and I cleaned, packed and laughed as the last of my belongings were placed in boxes, labelled and taken out to the car throughout the day. Five p.m. rolled around faster than I expected as my mind was distracted. I forgot all about my troubles momentarily, feeling lighter as we reminisced about high school whilst carefully sealing my belongings in cardboard boxes.

I check the time, glancing at my watch to ensure I can make the short drive and arrive on time at the venue at six p.m. I carefully gather my camera, folio and equipment to prepare for the final shoot. As I shrug the last of my belongings over my shoulder I turn, and genuinely smile at Madison and Skylar. Their friendship and support has been endless, I am indebted to them and only hope that someday, I can return their kindness tenfold.

"See you at home." Madison smiles as she embraces me and kisses me on the cheek goodbye. "Thank you." I breathe as she waltzes out the door happily, launching herself into Cruize's car as he sits idle in the driveway, waiting patiently for her to emerge.

The girls are flying home tonight, although I will be driving home. We filled my car to the brim with my belongings at my insistence that I would enjoy the drive. It's over a thousand miles away, although I think subconsciously I made the decision as I just needed more time. Time and space to contemplate *everything*, and put on a brave face before I re-emerge home.

"See you soon sweetie, I love you." Skylar giggles as she hugs me tightly like it's the last time I'm ever going to see her.

"Skylar, I will be home soon. Please don't worry and thank you for everything you have done for me. I can never repay you for the all the ways you have helped me," I announce, meaning more than was actually said but she doesn't linger as she ushers me into my car for the photo shoot.

Isabelle

I arrive at the required address exactly ten minutes early.

I pull the car neatly into one of the empty parking spaces out the front of the location and pause for a moment, taking a deep breath in. Everything is hard these days; smiling, talking, going places... living. I continue to take a few deep breaths and finally exit the car. "You can do this," I chant to myself as I gather my things and my thoughts. I steel myself and put on a brave face, attempting to wash away all of my other emotions with a robust smile.

"Moving away will be the best thing for me," I confirm silently in my head. "With ocean as my sound board, and the motion of the waves to carry away my thoughts with the tide – I will not sink. I will learn to swim." I chime mentally, cheering myself on for encouragement as I look up at the shop front. "Memphis Music." I huff. "Why on earth is this place so important?" I fume, my emotions shifting from positive to negative in the blink of an eye. "Of course, it's a music store as the devil wants to push me a little further into the depths of hell." I seethe as I lock the car and wrestle with my emotions.

I cling to my satchel tighter as it hangs over my shoulder and I make my way to the front door. The lights are on, illuminating the store, so I gather my professional facade and push gently on the door. I hear the bells chime happily overhead as I enter and stand tentatively inside the store.

"Hello," I call into the shop. "My name is Isabelle. I'm here for the photo shoot," I continue.

"This place is really beautiful," I breathe as I scan the room with the eyes of an eagle.

The walls are lined with guitars, memorabilia and a vast array of beautiful instruments. I'm compelled to move forward, my curiosity winning as I absorb the fascinating artefacts. A large solid counter and glass display cabinets grace the back of the store, drawing me closer with intrigue as they hold the most precious items. I make my way slowly through the shop, enchanted by every object – but careful not to touch anything.

"Hello Isabelle." A familiar voice enters my ears and my heart skips a beat.

"Walter, is that you?" I whisper, my voice barely audible.

"Yes Isabelle, come in love, take a seat," he replies warmly.

"I don't understand?" I stammer. "Did he put you up to this?" I ask confused. Memories and images instantly flood my brain of Maverick; his beautiful smile, his dangerously intoxicating scent, his mesmerising sounds, his ravishing chaos and absolutely everything that is Maverick Black.

I can almost feel him breathing down my neck, whispering his utmost secret and pleasurable desires in my ear as I turn to flee; my first instinct is to run. I cannot deal with this right now. He cannot shatter my heart into a thousand pieces then walk away and expect me to be okay. "Isabelle, please give me a moment," Walter pleads, sensing my hesitation. "He loves you Isabelle, more than you know. Please," he pleads desperately again.

Walters face appears sad, he looks worn and aged since I have seen him last. He looks years older in a matter of a few months with an aura of sadness surrounding him. "Has Maverick done this?" I think silently.

Thoughts race wildly through my head, images and memories. I can barely breathe as I bend over with my hands resting on my knees supporting me. I take deep breaths in and out, attempting to keep my anxiety at bay.

"Isabelle," Walter states. "I have something for you, please sit down, I won't be a minute," he urges as he ushers me into the stool perched at the counter. I turn around slowly, dazed and confused as I prop myself up, moving mechanically to sit down at the counter and slump my satchel unceremoniously on the floor.

"Is this a dream?" I wonder. "Maverick made his choice and it certainly wasn't me, so why am I here?" I think to myself. "I feel like I can't carry any more weight upon my shoulders as the burden already encumbers me with each step I take." I consider this as my breathing evens out. "I've been torn apart, broken into miniscule pieces and left behind with a shattered heart. I don't deserve to be reminded again and again of him," I think angrily as my pain claws its way back to the surface.

"Baby girl, life won't get easier because you wish it. The world will get harder; know that, but also know that you will only get stronger, each and every time you're faced with adversity. Your capacity to deal with the challenges on your journey will expand with time – making you the strongest person in your world." Flynn chimes through my memories as I feel a crushing pain deep inside my chest.

I feel entirely broken. Beautifully broken and I am not ashamed of that. It is nothing to hide behind as I find my universe again and reflect thoughtfully on Flynn's words. Although, it's moments like these, when I am pushed to the very edge of my limits – I only wished someone was here with me, to fight alongside me in my journey.

"Here," says Walter, interrupting my erratic thoughts. He lifts a black case onto the counter, pulling me out of my trance for a brief moment. I recognise the shape instantly, it's a guitar case, and brand new by the looks of it.

"Walter, why are you giving me this?" I ask

"Honey, Maverick asked me to make this for you a long time ago, he wanted to give you something special as words don't always come easy love. I made this for you, and he asked me to give it to you," Walter explains.

I stare at the case. "Please Isabelle," Walter pleads.

I glance up at Walter. "Should I open it?"

Walter is such a kind and decent human, I know he would have spent hours, days, weeks and months painstakingly making this for me. I recognise we are both hurting right now, tied to the same person – inexplicably intertwined. Walter nods as I slowly run my fingers along the hard-shell case and down the clasps holding it firmly shut. I flick one buckle, then another. I continue unclasping the locks until there is nothing left between me and the contents hidden safely inside the case.

I sit motionless for what feels like a perpetuity.

I can hear the clock ticking routinely on the wall, the only sound in the shop apart from the occasional car passing outside. Walter moves slowly and silently away from the counter and out towards the back of the shop.

I think back to Flynn telling me how stubborn and determined I am. *"You need to let people in Isabelle."* His words run through my head as he whispers into my thoughts, *"Open it princess,"* he encourages over and over again. I can imagine Flynn smirking as he watches me, like a parent on Christmas day, waiting to see their kids delight as they unwrap a special gift.

I slowly lift the top of the guitar case upright until it can support itself on the back hinges and I peer inside. I inhale sharply, holding my breath as my hands instinctively race to my face. The magnificent beauty of the guitar that lays perfectly inside steals my heart instantly. It's a distinctive looking acoustic guitar made from a combination of highly compressed wood fibers. A tiny blue bird is embossed on the guitar just below the sound hole, almost like it's waiting for the music to escape.

It's so incredibly beautiful. I think of the passion and quality that has been imbued into the guitar as tear escapes my eye and streams softly down my face, such a gesture is unimaginable. I am utterly speechless, my voice lost with such a divine gift from someone who ruined me completely.

I delicately lift the guitar from its resting place, and position it on my lap as I begin to cry quietly, waves of emotions rolling through me. It's inscribed *songbird* beautifully in blue italics underneath the bird, and I know that part is distinctively Maverick. Maverick is the only one who called me songbird, and it feels beyond special reading the unique inscription, meant only for me. I feel him deep in my soul, he's a significant part of me, and it's missing. I feel like my heart is breaking all over again as I lightly strum the guitar, feeling my heart shattering into a million tiny pieces with every sweep of the strings.

Through my tears, I notice a shimmering white envelope in the bottom of the guitar case. It reads *Songbird x* handwritten on the front of the envelope in a rich blue ink. A whimper escapes me, knowing whatever is in that envelope – Maverick wrote it.

I lift the envelope and feel the handwriting with my fingers, I run them delicately back and forth over the envelope. I slowly turn the envelope over and slide my fingers under the seal to open it. I'm careful not to tear a single part of the envelope, I'm not sure why, but a part of me imagines that if it rips, then I will wake up. I will be dramatically ripped away from this very moment, all of it – a vivid dream.

Maverick

I stare at the blank page for hours. "How to write my feelings on this piece of paper?" My thoughts are clear, but actually articulating them via a pen and paper is not something that comes easy to me.

"This should be easy considering I sing everyday about people, love, heartbreak, happiness and sadness, but I feel that no words will ever be good enough for her. Nothing I write on this page will even come close to the depths of my feelings for her." I consider this as every memory of her flashes vividly through my head.

"I don't have much time, I need to think." I worry as I stare at the blank page again. I snatch the papers and pen from the table and head to the door, my combat boots feel like they weigh a thousand pounds as I stomp down the steps of the warehouse.

I reach the park where Isabelle takes most of her photos.

I lie in the lush green grass close to the water and feel instantly relived. I lay there for hours and simply stare at the blue sky and the moving clouds. I feel at peace here, it helps clears my head of all the noise and clutter that has taken up residence in my brain. I think subconsciously I also ended up by the lake as I feel closer to Isabelle, just by being here.

I filter through my memories; I see her smiling happily as people jog past, I see her breathing in the fresh air with a genuine gratefulness, I see her laughing as children play excitedly on the grass, I see her walking along the water, shoes in hand and her bare feet whispering along the sand.

"God, I never meant to hurt her, and would give up anything and everything – just to see her one more time." I think about this sadly, knowing that it's certainly impossible.

Maverick

Dear Isabelle,

I lay here in the park staring at the sky for hours, wishing it was you here beside me.
   You have changed my life infinitely, and I am struggling to find the right words to express how much you mean to me.
   I am completely in love with you Isabelle. I know I should have said it sooner, but know that you are the only one for me. I will always be yours Isabelle – forever in my heart.
   My existence feels barren without you, you are my entire god damn universe and my reason to breathe songbird. You showed me peace when I was angry. You shared your love when I was alone and you were my light when I was lost.
   I never meant to hurt you Isabelle.
   Please always remember that, and know I would give everything I have left just to make sure another tear never leaves your eyes, you never feel an inch of sadness and I could protect you forever. I only wish I had enough time to explain everything to you. I am sorry Isabelle, I tried, but I just couldn't find the words, and now it's too late.
   You deserve to be happy, you deserve to be free Isabelle. You are a beautiful soul; so passionate, so caring, so eager to live and learn and yet so incredibly stubborn. So, I'm telling you:
   Open your heart and let go, let life in and live your wildest dreams Isabelle. Dream big and don't stop, chase those dreams

and most importantly – love. Fall in love with yourself again and the very essence of you. Love fiercely each and every minute of every day.

I have to go Isabelle, but I want you to remember – life is short songbird, embrace every moment and be happy. Flood the world with your heart, soul, kindness and compassion and be loved in return. Live an extraordinary life.

Please don't cry, be strong beautiful and no matter how hard things get, please don't ever give up hope. I will always be with you.

I will be your angel now.
I love you Isabelle, until we meet again,
Yours eternally, Maverick. x

Isabelle

I exhale loudly, the profound impact is indescribable.

I wipe the tears away from my eyes and attempt to place my heart back into my chest. A beautiful smile crosses my face as I realise Flynn was right all along with his words of wisdom, *"Isabelle, you are loved. You are so incredibly special, yet you are the only person in the universe who cannot see this. If you truly love Maverick then fight for him. Fight with everything you have and never give up hope."*

I grab the letter tightly, holding it close to my chest whilst I race to the front of the store. "Walter!" I yell, "I have to go, I have to find him." I finish hurriedly. Walter rushes out from behind the door, emerging from the storeroom.

"Isabelle, wait! It's too late, he's gone," he shouts.

"Walter, I will find him, I have to find him." I smile as I rattle the old glass door open excitedly as I exit. The bells jingle happily overhead as I race outside and into my car.

The engine purrs to life as I start my car, my heart is pounding and tears are streaming down my face. "Maverick is letting me go. I must find him, I *will* fight for us." I smile through my tears.

I park haphazardly across the road from Mavericks' warehouse and race up the stairs two steps at a time. I pause to catch my breath at the top of the staircase, wiping my eyes before I bang frantically on the front door. I have no idea what I'm going to say, I just know I need to be here, I want to be here.

I hear footsteps approaching the door. I stand electrified, the fire once again pulsing through my veins as a few seconds later the door creaks open cautiously.

My happiness fades instantly – it's her. The girl from the shower, the beautiful, tall and mysterious stranger that emerged from Mavericks bathroom the last time I mustered up the courage to talk to him. I observe her in silence for a moment. She looks as though she has been crying with dark circles under her eyes, her skin looks pale and almost translucent. She is wearing no make-up and her dark hair is tied up messily on top of her head.

I stare at her, not knowing what to say in this moment. "Isabelle." She breathes. "Please come in, I'm Arizona. Mavericks sister," she states as she pulls me in for a warm embrace.

"Mavericks sister?" I think as I take a step back after a moment and stare at her silently.

"Jesus, I'm such a complete asshole. I ran from Maverick even though he told me it wasn't what I thought." I cringe inwardly. It feels awkward with her hugging me after my last performance when I seen her in the warehouse, although she appears to be entirely at ease with me in her presence.

"Come in please," she gestures.

I tentatively step inside the warehouse and peer around the ground floor. Noticeably – there are no traces of Maverick and I sigh, internally disheartened. Boxes are strewn across the floor and the place no longer resembles Maverick. It feels cold, vacant, and empty like a void.

"I'm so sorry Isabelle, he's gone," she whispers as she stares at the unlit fire and then out towards the balcony doors.

"Where has he gone Arizona?" I ask urgently. "I must find him," I plea.

Arizona turns around, tears streaming down her face. "He didn't tell you, did he?" she asks.

"Come, sit down Isabelle." She motions quietly for the couch in front of the fireplace before I can respond. Her pain is so real, it is overwhelming the sadness pouring out of her, etched painfully in each of her words and I start to panic. I feel distressed and fearful of what is to come. I also don't know how to help her as my own emotions run rampant with a stampede of thoughts rallying throughout my mind. I want to reach out and embrace her, offer her some miniscule level of comfort, but I don't, the threat of the unknown has me conflicted as I slowly ease myself onto the couch, sitting motionless waiting for what it is she has to tell me.

"Please Arizona, he didn't tell me what? What is it?" I ask, pleading desperately.

Arizona takes a deep breath and sits beside me on the couch, turning to face me as she wipes her tears away and begins to speak. "Isabelle, Maverick was diagnosed two years ago with a an illness, one where there is no definite cure for all." She stops and takes a breath and stares out the window again. "The survival rates are incredibly low for five years and even lower for ten years," Arizona elaborates softly.

"We were completely gutted and heartbroken as a family, unable to function, unable to come to terms with his diagnosis as a unit. An illness that has no logic, no rhyme or reason as to who it chooses in its path of absolute destruction." She explains as if delivering an ancient brutal roman punishment sentence upon another.

"Maverick spiralled out of control after the diagnosis into the deepest, darkest recesses of his mind, so deeply ingrained within himself that we didn't know how to pull him out of the despair – not even me," she tells me softly.

"Mavericks moods spiralled more and more with each day into a dangerous and chaotic state as he lost interest in everything, even his music. His agitation continued to grow tenfold with his irritability and he lost the ability to find solace in anything anymore. Maverick lacked concentration due to the intense headaches and this was coupled with his incessant insomnia. It all collided, and his only wish was to entirely isolate himself. Maverick relentlessly shut his entire world out."

"Maverick unreservedly refused treatment and took off, moving from place to place. He ran from us Isabelle. Maverick decided to run as far away as he could muster to escape everyone, and his diagnosis." Arizona explains with the weight of this burden bearing heavily down upon her shoulders.

"You see Isabelle," she continues, "he went to a very dark place in his life. Maverick entirely blamed himself for the pain he had caused to others as a result of his diagnosis." She exhales. "God, our family, our friends and the entire universe is with him – every single step of the way, but he is the only one so blindsided that he cannot see it." Arizona sighs and sits motionless, staring at the cold, unlit fire dejectedly.

"His only wish," Arizona continues as my own words choke up within my chest, unable to be formulated or released as she pauses. My tears flow freely and my heart shatters as I consider the depths of Mavericks pain. "…was that that he wanted to die alone." Arizona whispers. She wipes the tears that continue to flood her own eyes and takes in a deep breath. "Maverick decided that he didn't want his family to see him suffer and he knew any treatment may not work."

"Mavericks gone Isabelle."